Praise for Cat Johnson's
Model Soldier

"Fun and intense and sweet and so much more would describe this addition to Cat Johnson's Red, Hot and Blue series...the romance was fabulous and the characters awesome."

~ *Night Owl Reviews*

"...deliciously alpha soldiers, slightly love-crazed advertising executives, and heart-pounding adventure on the edge of the war torn Middle East..."

~ *Sizzling Hot Book Reviews*

Look for these titles by
Cat Johnson

Now Available:

Rough Stock

Studs in Spurs
Unridden
Bucked
Ride
Hooked
Flanked

Red, Hot, & Blue
Trey
Jack
Jimmy
Jared
Cole
Bobby
A Few Good Men
A Prince Among Men

Print Collections
Red Blooded
Smalltown Heat

Model Soldier

Cat Johnson

Samhain Publishing, Ltd.
11821 Mason Montgomery Road, 4B
Cincinnati, OH 45249
www.samhainpublishing.com

Model Soldier
Copyright © 2013 by Cat Johnson
Print ISBN: 978-1-61921-515-3
Digital ISBN: 978-1-60928-854-9

Editing by Heidi Moore
Cover by Angela Waters

First Samhain Publishing, Ltd. electronic publication: December 2012
First Samhain Publishing, Ltd. print publication: November 2013

Dedication

This book is humbly dedicated to my military muses.

Sean, for letting me steal his images, his words and his inspiration from his multiple deployments to Afghanistan. To his soldiers, who often labor unappreciated for all they do.

Janelle, for having the toughest job on earth, that of military wife, and for cheerfully answering all of my many questions and sharing her husband's limited time with me.

Chilly, the man of few words, for loaning a few choice ones to me regarding his time in Kandahar. Peavler, for being my go-to answer guy at all hours. And finally Gary, for his continued support of both my writing and me.

As with all of my military novels, any inaccuracies or liberties taken with the facts are purely my own.

"Out of every one hundred men, ten shouldn't even be there, eighty are just targets, nine are the real fighters, and we are lucky to have them, for they make the battle. Ah, but the one, one is a warrior, and he will bring the others back."
— Heraclitus, 500 B.C.

Chapter One

Late 2007

Army Staff Sergeant David *Hawk* Hawkins kneeled and surveyed the barren wasteland of the icy terrain ahead. Gusts of brisk winter air howled across the desolation. The frigid area was vacant of all life save his squad. Exhaling, Hawk watched his breath freeze before him in mid-air.

With the raise of a gloved hand, he signaled his men. The silent wraiths emerged from the ground, cloaked in the arctic mist. The only sign of their corporeal selves was the barely discernible crunch of snow beneath boots. Upon his sign, Hawk's squad stealthily approached their final destination on the side of the mountain.

He was beginning to feel as though his many sins had come to bear and his sentence was this God-forsaken place. This mountain had become his personal Hell.

Hawk decided to err on the side of caution and signaled for a short halt as he considered the juggernaut before them. Through frozen lips, he whispered as softly as a lover's caress into his radio, "Bravo team, you're on overwatch. Alpha team, move out."

As they'd traveled this path to Hell over the past few hours—hours that seemed more like days—Hawk had divided his squad into two teams. Two entities separate yet bound together, one always supporting the other, providing security. He'd chosen his two best men to lead the teams, soldiers he would soon have to trust, not only with his own life, but also with the lives of them all.

Without a word, the two groups responded to his order by moving quickly and surely into position. The overwatch team opened fire into the rocks above. The belch of gunfire erupted and broke through the icy stillness. Tracers flew through the icy air like mad yellow jackets on a sunny day.

Hawk hit the rocky ground hard, knowing his body would pay later. But right now, he couldn't feel a thing, not while adrenaline surged through his veins as bullets struck the snow-covered rocks protecting him.

A too-familiar pop sounded.

"RPG! Take cover!" With no time for the radio, he shouted the warning.

The rocket propelled grenade cut a trail through the air, exploding nearby and showering him with debris as he lay behind cover.

While his men returned that less-than-friendly greeting with their own volley, he engaged the selector lever on his rifle with his thumb as his forefinger slipped onto the trigger. The scene seemed to move frame by frame to Hawk's eye as his brain and body, both on autopilot, processed and reacted to the situation.

Visually, Hawk traced the path the RPG had taken back to its owner whose fate was decided the moment he began to rise from cover before Hawk's sights.

Hawk squeezed the trigger.

Following the quick burst from his barrel, Hawk barely took the time to watch the man fall before he yelled, "Bravo team, maintain supportive fire."

With Bravo suppressing the enemy above, Hawk sprung from the ground and sprinted to join Alpha team. Diving behind protective cover, he knew he had to choose the next course wisely.

"Alpha team, follow me." Hawk issued the order as he began to maneuver far right in an attempt to flank his opposition. Using a partially covered route as the supportive fire kept the enemy pinned in place, he moved quickly.

"Shit," Hawk hissed as his boot slipped on the treacherous footing. Moving too rapidly in this terrain could mean a fall from what was in all probability a deadly height, while moving too slowly could give the enemy the advantage and mean his squad's demise.

After taking a calming breath that would hopefully reach down to steady his feet, Hawk ran. A few enemy shots peppered the path around him. There was no choice but to accept the risk and drive forward if he wanted to win this battle.

Through his headset, Hawk heard the good news that Bravo team had scratched two and continued to suppress the remaining enemy element. Two less bad guys to worry about as Alpha team got into place to assault the remaining opposition from the right.

Hawk waited until the last possible moment before he ordered, "B team. We're in position. Lift and shift fire." *And please try and not hit us.* He added a silent prayer to whatever godly force aided soldiers in battle that none of his men would fall to fratricide.

He saw the enemy scramble. Having been pinned down, they failed to see Hawk's approach until too late. As they attempted to swing their weapons to ward off the surprise attack to their right flank, they fell one by one. To their credit, or perhaps as a testament to their stupidity, none tried to surrender, but instead fought to the bitter end.

After a quick survey to ensure his own men were still alive and standing, a small smile crossed his ice-cold lips as he allowed himself barely a breath to enjoy the victory.

Many a dead man had learned too late not to celebrate prematurely. There was still much to do. "Bravo, establish security. Alpha, search the area."

His men, who up until this moment had been silent, efficient killers, suddenly transformed into jubilant boys, filling the air with whoops and chatter as soon as they had completed the quick job of checking the downed team and clearing the training weapons from them.

Shaking his head at their behavior, he didn't bother to correct them. This had been a training exercise, not an actual mission, so he supposed he could cut them some slack. They had been swift and the work was already done. Hawk called in to base to report the situation and do a bit of bragging of his own.

"Team One to Base. This is Hawk. Over."

"Go ahead, Hawk. Over."

"The enemy has been eliminated. Awaiting further orders. Over."

"Return to base for debriefing. Over," the disembodied voice told him.

"Copy that. Over and out." Hawk sighed and looked at the crimson-spotted snow surrounding him. He'd led his team to victory, but in what amounted to a glorified game of paintball. His only hope, when the time came many months in the future, was to bring all his men back from Afghanistan to their loved ones, alive and unscathed.

Well, perhaps that wasn't his only wish. He wouldn't mind something warm in his belly right now—coffee, food or whisky, any of the three would suffice. Hell, he wasn't picky. While he was wishing, he hoped the journey back down to base would be easier than the one here. There was no way it could be any worse.

As he and the team negotiated the frigid path to base, Hawk soon realized he couldn't have been more wrong.

"Fuck." Hawk lowered his head against the driving wind. He couldn't help thinking his protective facemask wasn't doing so great a job of protecting him at the moment.

"Sergeant?" Ryan Pettit questioned his comment. Pettit, Hawk's second in command and the man who'd led Alpha team that day, squinted against the sudden snow squall that blew tiny ice daggers into all their eyes.

"Nothing, Pettit. It's just I think I cursed us. I'd hoped the trip back down would be easy. This is what I get for that." Hawk shook his head at his foolishness.

His Alpha-team leader laughed. "Well, you know what they say. Put your hopes in one hand and shit in the other hand and see which one fills up fastest."

Hawk laughed at that jest.

Wally, aka Trent Wallace, his Bravo-team leader, emerged out of the blizzard from somewhere next to Pettit. He looked about as miserable as Hawk felt. Visibility was limited pretty much to the distance of his hand in front of his face. Thank God, they'd finished off the enemy before this thing hit.

"I thought it was wishes, not hopes. Put your wishes in one hand and shit in the other." Wally sounded like his mouth was frozen. They were all talking a little funny at the moment. Impending frostbite does that to a person.

13

"Hopes, wishes, same damn thing." Looking grim, Pettit swiped at his face with one gloved hand, knocking away the snow that had built up on his eyelashes and brows.

"Yeah. Pretty much." Hawk had to agree. Hopes, wishes, both were useless.

Starting to look like the abominable snowman himself, Hawk began feeling uncharacteristically superstitious, probably due to hypothermia and hunger. Then and there, he swore to himself he'd remember in the future not to do either, wishing or hoping. Not if this kind of torture was the result.

Thanks to the sudden storm, the journey down the mountain took them twice as long as the trip up. The only solace being that they walked away victorious and without any losses. When they finally arrived at base, Hawk gladly sent his men back to their temporary lodging to eat and get warm. Meanwhile, he sat and waited, not so gladly, to be debriefed by the commanding training officer in charge of this shindig.

The man was taking his sweet damn time too, long enough that Hawk had the opportunity to lean his head back against the wall in the warm office, close his eyes and review the day, his life, his future...

This much reflection was definitely evidence that he was deliriously tired. As his thoughts drifted aimlessly, he couldn't help but wonder where the hell the time had gone.

It seemed as if he'd just gotten back to Germany from his third deployment in Iraq. Yet here he was, in the field once more, in the freaking Alps no less, for a mission-readiness exercise. But he'd do whatever it took, even freezing his ass off in the Alps, to prepare his new unit before they headed out again, this time for Afghanistan. The Kabul Province, to be exact.

He'd thought Iraq had been bad, but from what he'd heard, Afghanistan made Iraq look like the frigging French Riviera. Awaiting them in the far mountainous outskirts of the city of Kabul would be a few makeshift shacks for living areas, a generator or two and a small cooking area. That was the extent of what he'd been told they could expect to find in the way of comfort.

Supplies would have to be flown in by chopper to reach them. He'd heard there had been improvements and that more may be done before he arrived. One could only hope. Not that it mattered how sparse or unimproved conditions were, they would still complete their assigned mission.

He and his men had been so busy the past few months, using their combined experience from their tours in the sandbox to help train the guys in other units at the garrison in Hohenfels, they'd pretty much gotten the shaft for time to train themselves for this new deployment. At least until today, when this last-minute training in the Alps had been thrown at them.

Hawk hoped they all wouldn't pay the price for lack of preparedness once they hit Afghanistan. There, the platoon would be doing dismounted ops the majority of the time, far from assistance and farther from home.

But he wasn't in Afghanistan yet. Instead, he sat here at base camp on the mountain infamous for breaking people, trying to recover from one of the hardest damn training exercises he'd ever been through. In fact, he'd hardly thought about his upcoming deployment in hours since the mock "enemy" force he'd faced today demanded every last scrap of his attention.

The current situation made last week's two days of training and live-fire exercises in the field back at his home base at Hohenfels look like a walk in the park, even with the freezing temperatures and five inches of snow on the ground. Compared to the conditions here, that workout had been nothing.

The German Army prepared on the very same rocky terrain where Hawk had trained today. Many areas reportedly had up to four feet of snow. Hawk could only think that the Army sent them here because these were the same conditions they could expect to find in the mountains separating Afghanistan and Pakistan. The same region where Osama bin Laden's boys still maintained a stronghold in spite of all the good guys' efforts.

Today, Hawk's unit had faced some supposedly elite Special Forces sent in by Central Command to play the part of the bad guys to ready them for Afghanistan.

CentCom's handpicked golden boys were good, but not good enough. Hawk's squad, ten soldiers plus himself, had grown to be one hell of a force. Good enough to whip this Task Force Zeta's ass up and down the side of that God-forsaken mountain.

The sound of a door opening broke into Hawk's thoughts. His eyes flew open in time to see the black-clad, gray-haired training commander enter the room.

Hawk took the commander's offered hand and shook it while trying to ignore how much effort it took to even raise his arm from his side.

"Sergeant Hawkins. You did well up there today." Commander Miller, the man in charge of this show, greeted him.

They did well? They'd done fucking great, was more like it. But instead of voicing that opinion, Hawk inclined his head and accepted the compliment.

"I can't take credit for the complete molding of them, sir. I have one strong team leader and the other is decent. He's a bit rough around the edges, but I'm working to fix that. Together, the team leaders and I have trained the rest of the Joes."

He'd gotten them to where he needed them to be, acting together, their movements fluid. They were efficient killers when needed, capable of identifying the enemy amongst a crowd and engaging only those who were combatants. Following his orders without question or complaint and taking down the bad guys without hesitation or regret.

Commander Miller smiled and elbowed the man who had followed him into the room. "Damn. I guess I shouldn't have told you guys to go easy on them. I would have loved to see what they could really do. What do you think, Dalton?"

"The guys would have loved to play full out, sir. I thought Bull would lose his mind having to hold back like that. Maybe next time." The Task Force Zeta Operative Hawk recognized as leading the opposing team in today's exercise shrugged casually.

Hawk swung his gaze from this Dalton guy to the commander. "Excuse me?"

"Yes, Sergeant?" Miller raised a brow.

Shaking his head in disbelief, Hawk practically sputtered with anger. "You had your team hold back?"

"Nothing to worry about, soldier. I would never expect your squad to compete against Zeta when they play full out. Go and get some rest. And again, good job up there today, Sergeant." Miller slapped Hawk on the shoulder then turned to go.

Anger-fueled and breaking all protocol, Hawk grabbed Miller's arm. "Run the exercise again." Then he added a quick, "Sir," and then a, "please." Although a little sojourn in the brig for insubordination would provide him some much needed rest, Hawk figured it was probably best to avoid it if possible.

Miller shook his head. "You won, son. There's no need."

The commander's eyes lowered briefly to Hawk's hand, still on him. Hawk dropped his hold immediately, but not the subject.

"There is no victory for me if your team didn't go full out. Do you really think the insurgents in Afghanistan will be holding back when they face my men?" Hawk stifled anything else he might have wanted to say before he did end up in the brig.

An amused look crossed Miller's face as his gaze moved from Hawk to his team leader for this exercise.

"Dalton?" Miller questioned the man with one word.

"He does have a point there, commander. And our guys would really enjoy being able to kick some ass unrestrained." A cocky grin crossed pretty-boy Dalton's face, just begging to be knocked off with the help of Hawk's fist.

"All right, Sergeant. I'll call Gordon back at the rear to confirm nothing's come up that requires the team's immediate attention. But barring that, you get your wish, soldier. I'll see you and your squad here at zero-four-thirty."

Hawk's men were not going to be happy when he informed them they'd be traipsing around outside in God only knew how much fresh powder at zero-dark-thirty instead of dreaming in their racks. All because of him and his damn pride. Hawk mouthed a silent curse.

Dalton noticed and laughed. "You walked right into that one, Sergeant Hawkins."

Yeah, he'd really like to slug this guy all right. But for now, he had to go break the news to his men that they were not only spending one more night and day on this mountain, but they wouldn't be doing a hell of a lot of sleeping during it either.

The commander's words echoed in his head. *"You get your wish, soldier."* Hawk's final thought as a smiling Dalton closed the door of the office behind him was that he really had to remember to stop wishing.

Chapter Two

The problem with mothers was this—you had to love them, even when you didn't like them very much.

Annoyed, Emily Price considered this as she felt her hand go numb from her tight grip on the phone receiver.

Meanwhile, her mother continued to regale her with tales of exactly how wonderful Emily's flawless sister Lily was for taking her shopping the other day, which Emily never did.

Perhaps that was because Lily and their mother both lived in Chicago, while Emily lived and worked, very hard she might add, in New York.

She didn't bother bringing up that small yet pertinent fact. It would only restart another familiar ritual battle, that being why didn't Emily move back home or at the very least visit more often?

For what? So she could feel inadequate next to her sister? Perfect Lily, whose hair had always been blonder than Emily's, whose grades had always been higher, whose boyfriends had always been nicer...

"Emily Rose. I can tell you're not listening to me."

Uh, oh. Had she forgotten to mindlessly respond at what her mother felt was the appropriate time during her diatribe?

"Are you playing on that computer of yours again while I'm trying to talk to you?" The accusation in her mother's tone came loud and clear through the receiver held in Emily's death grip.

Playing. Yeah, because working for the busiest woman on the face of the earth, or at least on Madison Avenue, was all fun and games.

Resorting to base instinct as she held onto her temper and her sanity by the tips of her fingernails, Emily knew the time had come for fight or flight. She had to choose one and soon, because she wasn't going to make it on this phone call one minute more without blowing up.

"I'm sorry, Mom. My boss really needs me. I've got to go. Call you back soon. Love you. Bye."

She managed to stifle the long, loud, pent-up groan waiting in her throat until after she'd slammed the receiver down into the cradle, using a bit more force than necessary to disconnect the call. Emily took one more glance at the display to make sure she really had totally and completely hung up before letting her head drop to the desk.

After a bit, the slow, steady thudding of Emily's head banging against the desktop ceased, leaving only the soft sound of her boss's snicker.

"How come I always have to be the bad guy who makes you hang up on your mother? I think I'm insulted. I'm a nice person. I would never do that for real."

"Oh, shut up." Emily groaned, forehead still pressed against the cool, smooth wooden surface. "You're an only child, Katie. You can't possibly understand what I go through with my mother and sister."

"Now, now. I'm dating a man with eight siblings, so I've gotten quite an education from BB in this area."

Billy Bob Dalton, only the hottest as well as nicest man on earth, was Katie's boyfriend. Another reason to hate her besides her lack of siblings. She had the perfect boyfriend.

Brushing the hair out of her face, Emily glanced past tousled blonde bangs and noticed her boss's face had turned deathly white.

Sitting straight, she was about to ask what was wrong when Katie jumped from her seat. Her boss pressed one hand over her mouth and ran from the room.

Frowning and concerned, Emily leapt to follow her. "Katie?"

"I'll be fine." The muffled response was all Emily heard before the restroom door slammed shut.

Once Katie emerged, she could interrogate her further about the sudden departure. She perched on the edge of Katie's desk to wait when a distinct scent caught her attention. Searching for the source, Emily discovered something very strange sitting innocently amid her boss's cluttered mess. Suddenly, it all started to make sense.

She was still leaning on Katie's desk holding the suspicious object in question when the ailing woman finally returned.

"What is this?" Emily held up her evidence. She'd probably spoken sterner than she should to a woman who was obviously suffering.

Katie's face paled once again. "Um, that's my coffee mug."

"Yes, it is your coffee mug." Emily nodded. "And you love coffee. You can't live without coffee. You grind your own beans for God's sake. So why, oh why, is there tea in your coffee mug? Caffeine-free herbal tea, no less."

To prove her point, Emily sniffed the minty aroma, already suspecting she knew the answer.

Striding forward but still visibly woozy, Katie grabbed the mug from Emily's hands. "A person can try something new once in a while. Can't she?"

Katie sat heavily in the desk chair, slumping rather than displaying her usual perfect posture that went along with the perfect rest of her.

Apparently sensing she was still under Emily's scrutiny, Katie avoided eye contact, studiously shuffling a few papers on her crowded desk. "Where is that file for the Army ad campaign? You know, we still need to find a model for that."

"Stop trying to change the subject." Emily scowled at the obvious diversionary tactic.

Still not looking up, Katie shook her head. "Jeez. An inquisition over a little cup of mint tea."

With a new idea, Emily made her way to the small kitchenette in the office. There they stored the necessities in case they had to throw together a quick show of hospitality for some big client or talent on the spur of the moment. The fridge was always stocked with bottled water, both bubbly and flat, an assortment of fruit and cheeses, champagne and chardonnay.

What Emily needed was in the cabinet. She reached past the bottles of red wine on the lower shelf to grab a box of unopened, plain water crackers from above.

After dropping the box on the desk, Emily crossed her arms and stood over Katie. "Eat some. It will help. My sister couldn't get enough of those when she was pregnant."

Katie's gaze shot up and a guilty expression marred her face. "How'd you know?"

"Hm. I don't know. Turning green and running for the bathroom. No more caffeine for the coffee junky..." Emily raised a brow and ticked off the proof on her fingers. She paused and waited for Katie's imminent confession.

"I'm so sorry I didn't tell you. I haven't told anyone yet except BB."

"Why? You know you can trust me. You can tell me anything and I'd take it to the grave. That's what assistants and friends are for."

Tears glistened in Katie's eyes. "I know." She paused and glanced around the office until Emily handed her a tissue from the box on the corner of the desk behind her. "Thank you. And it's not that I don't trust you. It's my body I don't trust. Em, I'm forty. I'm too old to be pregnant with my first child."

"No, you're not. How old was BB's mom when she had him?"

"That doesn't count. He was her ninth."

"That doesn't matter. And besides, things are different nowadays. Women are having babies into their fifties. Modern medicine has all these tests and stuff. It's perfectly safe."

Katie laughed tearfully. "This coming from a girl in her twenties with nice young eggs and a good firm uterus."

Emily rolled her eyes as Katie continued. "I'm just so afraid. BB doesn't want to show me how excited he is because he knows how worried I am, but I know he is totally in love with the idea of being a dad. Em, what if I miscarry?"

"BB is totally in love with you, and he will continue to be no matter what happens."

"I know that, when I can think straight. I'm just so emotional and irrational lately." Wiping her eyes, Katie looked up. Her gaze met Emily's. "I'm sorry to lay this all on you."

"Don't you dare apologize. I'm here for you. You know that. I'm sorry you're feeling so badly. Where's BB right now? I'll cover work for you if you want to fly down to the base and visit him. That might make you feel better."

Being in the arms of a hottie like BB would surely make Emily feel better.

Katie laughed at that. "No, no need for you to cover for me. He's in the Alps. That flight is a bit too long for me at the moment. There wouldn't be enough barf bags on the plane for a trip as far as Germany."

Emily bit her lip. "Were you supposed to tell me that he's in Germany? Isn't where he goes top secret?"

BB was some sort of super-secret Special Operative.

"If it was classified he wouldn't have been able to tell me, so I couldn't have told you, now could I?" Katie raised a brow.

That sounded reasonable enough, but working with the military on their marketing had been a lesson in rules, both rational and not. "Mmm. I guess so. Can I ask one more thing?"

"Sure." Katie tried to break into the cracker box as she began to pale again.

After watching her struggle with the cellophane wrapping for about a second, Emily grabbed the box out of her hands, tore it open and handed it back. "Are there terrorists hiding in the Alps now too?"

Katie chewed and swallowed a cracker and then shook her head. "Not that I know of, but I suppose anything is possible nowadays. He said it's just a training exercise. Commander Miller brought BB's task force in to help train some Army guys. No big deal, he said. Nothing to worry about..." Katie's voice trailed off.

Long-distance relationships were tough. This one with BB was even more so given his occupation. Emily knew Katie did worry, each and every time her boyfriend and his mysterious black-clad task-force buddies disappeared for an undetermined amount of time to parts unknown. With a baby added to the

Cat Johnson

mix that worry and the frequent separations would only be worse for Katie.

That raised the next question that had yet to be answered. "What are you two going to do, you know, about getting married? I mean it's totally cool if you have a baby and don't get married. People do that all the time."

Katie laughed. "Don't worry. BB asks me to marry him every day. Sometimes twice a day."

"And you haven't said yes yet?" What was wrong with this woman?

"I finally did a few days ago." Katie smiled weakly. "He wore me down. Either that, or it was the hormones talking."

Emily clapped her hands together. She didn't care what had caused it, as long as it happened. "Yay! A wedding to plan. I love weddings."

"Hang on just a minute. I told him I'll only marry him if I make it past my third month without...you know."

"How far along are you now?"

Katie wasn't showing at all. Although now that Emily thought about it, did Katie's boobs seem to be straining the buttons on her shirt a bit?

"Eight weeks, closer to nine actually if the doctor calculated correctly. Only two months in and already I can barely ride in a car without getting carsick and my breasts hurt so badly they feel like they are about to explode."

Emily nodded in sympathy. "Yeah, my sister said that too. It doesn't last the whole time. Don't worry. But hey, you're more than two thirds of the way to that three-month marker. Besides, I have a good feeling about this. You wouldn't be having all these symptoms if that baby wasn't planted in there nice and firmly, right?"

26

Katie laughed. "I guess so."

"So we need to start planning, just in case. The good wedding places book up a year in advance or more—"

"No. No big plans. If this wedding happens, it will be small."

Emily let out a snort. "He has eight brothers and sisters. Exactly how small can it be?"

Katie groaned and slumped lower in her chair. For a high-powered New York marketing executive, her boss could sure be an introvert. "I know. That's why I told him I want to elope."

"Elope?" Emily's hopes fell.

"Relax. You'll be there, even if we end up at a drive-thru in Vegas married by an Elvis impersonator. I promise."

Well, that was something at least.

"Okay. Thanks." That she'd get to be there for the ceremony softened the disappointment a bit, but not enough. Emily thought longingly about all the missed opportunities to visit bridal shops and watch Katie try on long white, or perhaps off-white, dresses.

"Don't look so dejected, Em. You'll get your chance one day, and then you can plan as big a wedding as you want for yourself. I'll even help you."

"Yeah, sure, because the men are just knocking down the door to marry me." Emily rolled her eyes.

Katie shook her head. "I've never seen such a bright, attractive, kind-hearted woman spend so many Saturday nights without a date."

"Hey, that used to be my complaint about you," Emily reminded.

"Yes, it was, but now you don't have to worry about me or my love life anymore. I not only got myself a boyfriend, I also got knocked up. So go out and find yourself your perfect guy."

27

"Are any of BB's brothers single?" Good looks were genetic. The Dalton brothers would have to be at least as hot as BB.

"No, sorry. He's the youngest. The rest are all married off already."

Hmm, that was disappointing. "Any of his military guy friends single?"

"No military guys for you." There was a warning in Katie's voice.

Emily frowned. "Why do you say it like that?"

"Because one of us dating a Special Operative is enough stress. Believe me." Katie crossed her arms over her chest. "Go find your own guy. A nice civilian businessman or maybe a construction worker. The city is full of them both."

Maybe she didn't want a boring old normal guy.

"Some help you are." Feeling spiteful, Emily went to pour herself a nice, big steaming cup of caffeinated coffee. As payback she intended to drink it right in front of Katie. That would teach her boss for hogging the hot military men for herself.

Chapter Three

What the hell? Hawk frowned and counted the opposing team gathered at the rally point one more time.

"Problem?" There was that smug, pretty-boy smile again that Hawk had come to hate on Dalton's face.

Yeah, there was a frigging problem.

"Your team seems to have grown overnight." Hawk sounded much more casual than he felt about that fact.

He was sure his ten guys plus himself could take them, but that was still no reason to be happy Zeta was basically cheating by changing the rules mid-way into the game.

Pretty Boy Dalton nodded. "Ah. That. Yeah, when you told the commander you wanted Zeta to go all out, he called the rear and ordered the rest of the team over."

That put Zeta at a whopping seven men, not counting the commander who made eight. Two more than Hawk's men had faced during the prior day's exercise. On top of the extra manpower, they also had brought in some sophisticated computer shit. One of the new arrivals seemed to know how to use it as his fingers flew over the keys of not one but three laptops.

Noticing where Hawk's gaze rested, Dalton grinned. "Zeta wouldn't be Zeta without Matt Coleman, the computer god and all his equipment."

Extra guys and state-of-the-art equipment. Fucking cheaters. All Hawk and his squad had access to was what amounted to basic walkie-talkies, and they were happy when they worked correctly.

Hawk let out a sigh. He noticed Dalton seemed to be waiting for a response to what really hadn't been a question, but more of a boast that CentCom gave SpecOps better toys than Hawk's squad got.

Cocking his head, Hawk mustered a grin equal to Dalton's. "If your team thinks they need all that shit to beat us, then you go ahead and feel free to use it. My guys, however, don't need anything more than what we had yesterday to beat you. Just our wits and our skill."

Dalton broke into an all-out laugh. "I admire your confidence, Hawkins, but—"

Hawk watched as Dalton broke off mid-sentence and seemed to be hearing voices in his head. Pretty Boy's smile disappeared and the concentration became evident by the expression on his face.

When Dalton said softly, "BB here. Roger that," Hawk was sure of it. Pretty Boy was either crazy as a loon or actually talking to someone in his head.

"As I was saying, Hawkins, I admire your confidence, but there is no way your squad can beat Zeta."

When Dalton continued with his insults as if nothing out of the ordinary had just happened, Hawk really got pissed.

"What the hell was that all about?" Hawk pointed a finger at Dalton's ear to indicate the previous more-than-strange occurrence.

Although Hawk could see damn well that it was all an act, Dalton pondered the ceiling for a moment as he seemed to consider his answer carefully. Dalton was clearly fucking with him, playing mind games.

"Well, it is top secret, but I figure I can tell you since you're going to need all the help you can get today." Dalton looked extra cocky and tapped a finger to his right ear. "Cochlear communications implants. Whole team has them."

Fuck.

Hawk had heard rumors about SpecOps having communications devices actually surgically implanted in their frigging ears, but he'd thought it was bullshit. Maybe it was all still bullshit and Dalton was just messing with him.

But no, as Hawk glanced around the room he noticed more than one team member get the same glazed look and then respond to no one, including the damn training commander, Miller. One look at their supposed computer god told Hawk that Coleman was the puppet master, testing his toys, one by one. No wonder they'd needed him flown in for today.

"You still up for this?" Dalton donned a gleeful smile, his perfect teeth nearly blinding Hawk with their whiteness.

Hawk had never been one to back down from a challenge, no matter what the odds. "Hell yeah, I'm still up for this. You boys can talk to each other in your heads all you want, but you pampered SuperOps still won't be able to hold up against battle-toughened soldiers trained with real-world mission experience."

He watched as Dalton rose nicely to that challenge.

"Oh really? Would you like to make this a bit more interesting? A little wager perhaps?" Pretty Boy raised a brow.

Sure, Dalton would want to make a bet since he probably took home three times what Hawk did in military pay. In

31

addition to what was probably a huge basic allowance for housing while Hawk made due with living in the bachelor barracks.

Hawk shook his head and swallowed his pride. "I'm not much into betting for money, Dalton."

Pretty Boy nodded. "Fine. Not for money then. Something else."

Hawk frowned. "Like what?"

The other man shrugged and then, as if a bulb had been turned on in his tiny brain, Dalton's face lit up. He looked Hawk up and down appraisingly, even pausing at the muscles in his arms folded defiantly across his iron-pumped chest.

What the fuck? Dalton was checking him out? Was Pretty Boy one of those don't-ask, don't-tell kinds? Shit. What the hell was Hawk supposed to do about that? He sure as hell couldn't beat him up if he was a fancy pants.

Since Hawk had always been a straight shooter, as well as straight, he decided to come right out with it. "Listen, you're free to live your life however you want, but please tell me you're not hitting on me, Dalton. Because I gotta tell you, you couldn't be barking up a more wrong tree if you tried."

After a second of surprised silence, Dalton broke out laughing so hard he had to sober himself up before he could respond.

"No, Hawk. You're a real buff guy and all, but I'm as straight as you are and I've got a preg...uh...pretty girlfriend back home in the States to prove it. So no, we're not betting for a date with you." Dalton paused to chuckle one more time over that then continued. "But I did just think of a really good wager."

If they weren't betting for Hawk's masculine virtue, then what? "What you got in mind, Dalton? Out with it."

"There's this, um, special assignment that needs filling. It requires just the right man. Let's say that if your side loses, you have to take it, no questions asked." Dalton appeared rather pleased with himself.

Hawk frowned. "If this assignment is so special, why haven't you already filled it? Why doesn't anyone else want it?"

"I didn't say no one wanted it, just that it's special and needs the absolute perfect soldier to fill it. Believe it or not, Hawkins, that may be you."

"Well, I'm glad we both agree that I'm perfect, but I'm also on my way to Afghanistan for a year," Hawk reminded him. Probably more like eighteen months the way things had been going lately. "Tell me this. If we lose, which isn't likely, how could I possibly fulfill this assignment while deployed?"

"Easy. No problem at all. You can complete it before you go. Hell, you could probably even do it in Afghanistan if necessary. It's a quick one. A day. Two at most."

"You'll have to give me a little more information than that. I'd have to clear this with higher up first." What the fuck could this be about?

"Nope. No more info until the exercise is over and all the details for the assignment are ironed out. Besides, it will be so much more fun for both of us if it's a surprise." Dalton tilted a head toward the bank of laptops. "I'm sure Matt can get it cleared with your superiors by the time we get off that mountain, if you're game that is."

Coleman could get it approved with Hawk's commanding officers? How the fuck was that possible? Maybe it wasn't. This could all be more bullshit, in which case Hawk could agree to just about anything now and his superiors could shoot it down later, getting Hawk off the hook should he lose.

Even so, Hawk still had a nagging feeling he might have gone insane when he decided to agree to the gamble for this unknown assignment. "Oh, I'm game, Dalton. Not that we're going to lose, but I'll accept your little wager. One question remains however. What do I get if, no, *when* we win?"

"I'm sure your winning won't be an issue." Dalton smiled. "But just to be fair, what would you like?"

That stopped Hawk dead in his pride-filled shoes. "What do you mean, what would I like?"

"Exactly that. No games, Hawkins. If the universe shifts, hell freezes over, pigs fly and your group wins, what do you want?"

Cocky bastard. He'd show him. But still, Hawk couldn't come up with a thing. "I don't know," he admitted after an embarrassingly long moment spent in indecision.

Shit, why couldn't he think of anything really good? A keg of beer crossed his mind, but didn't seem like enough compared to the mystery assignment he'd have to take in exchange. A Humvee perhaps? Dalton had said anything, but what the hell would he do with it while he was deployed. Not to mention that when he finally got back Stateside, Hawk had a feeling if he never stepped foot inside one of those vehicles again it would be too soon.

"Want a suggestion?" Dalton asked after watching Hawk struggle.

"Sure." What the hell. Might as well see what Pretty Boy had to say.

"If Zeta loses, I'll get you a tryout for the teams."

Hawk didn't miss the smirk on Dalton's face as he emphasized the word *if.*

He raised a brow and then purposely played dumb. "What teams?"

"You know what teams." The words *smart ass* were unspoken but unmistakably present in Dalton's response.

Hawk had to smile. He was enjoying sparring with Pretty Boy.

"So, do we have a deal?" Dalton asked, one pretty brow raised.

David Hawkins in the SpecOps? Never. Not gonna happen, but it might be fun to see what the tryout was like. It would sure make a hell of a story if he made it and then turned them down.

After a breath, Hawk nodded and shook Dalton's extended hand. "Deal."

Dalton turned to leave when Hawk stopped him. "Hey, Dalton. Tell me one thing."

Pretty Boy paused. "Yeah?"

"This assignment. Is it something you'd be willing to do yourself?"

"You worried, Hawkins?" Dalton laughed.

"Not worried, Dalton. Just curious."

"Mmm hmm. Sure. But yeah, I've already done it. Believe me, I've already done it." Dalton turned to head for his task force commander, but not before looking back. "Oh, and Hawkins, besides the comm units, we've all got GPS implants too. So Matt can keep us informed of our positions during our real-world missions. I probably shouldn't have told you that either, but I figure your boys can use all the help you can get. See you up on the mountain."

Implanted tracking devices too? Well, fuck.

With that less-than-heartening farewell, the entire Task Force Zeta team disappeared as quickly as they'd arrived. He presumed they'd get into place on the mountain and await the arrival of Hawk's squad, who'd be walking into a pre-planned, computer-coordinated ambush like lambs to a slaughter.

Special assignment, here I come. Double fuck.

"Pettit! Report!" Pinned down by Zeta's gunfire for the past hour, Hawk had never felt so disconnected from his men nor as helpless as he did right then. Dalton's team seemed to be everywhere, and always one step ahead of Hawk and his men.

"Four of our men are down, Sergeant." Pettit's voice finally filtered through Hawk's earpiece. Hawk barely heard his Alpha-team leader over the noise, but what he'd heard wasn't good.

"Wally, what's Bravo team's status?" Hawk needed some good news at this point but there was no answer. "Wally. Dammit. Answer me!"

"I'm not allowed to talk if I'm dead, Hawk." Barely audible, Wally's voice came across the airwaves.

Shit.

More frustrated than before, Hawk shouted into his radio, "Bravo team. Someone who isn't dead, give me a damn report."

Radio silence gave him his answer. As far as this exercise was concerned, the entire Bravo team was deceased. That left himself and Pettit as sole survivors of his eleven-man squad. "Pettit?"

"Yes, Sergeant."

"What's your location?"

"I'm behind the rocks just to the east of you."

"What do you say if we're going to go out, we go out with a bang?"

"Are you talking about the Butch and Sundance offensive defense?" Pettit always was right on the money.

Butch Cassidy and the Sundance Kid, the squad's favorite movie. Sure, Butch and Sundance die, but they do it with style. "That's exactly what I'm thinking, Pettit."

"Roger that, Hawk. I'm ready."

He could hear the smile in Pettit's response. Doing something, even running toward your pretend death in a training exercise, was preferable to doing nothing at all.

"On my count of three then. One." Hawk checked his ammo before continuing. "Two. Three!"

Hawk flung himself out from behind the rocks, dove and rolled behind the closest cover. When the shots came at him again, he was in better position to see exactly where they came from and how best to get there.

Aware of Pettit falling almost immediately to enemy fire to his left, Hawk lobbed a grenade in the direction of the incoming volley that had taken his team leader out. While that explosion kept the shooter down, Hawk ran full out, head on toward the shooter, jumped on top of the rocks hiding his opponent and showered the man hidden there with a hail of gunfire before feeling the hit in his own back.

Even with the knowledge that he was, for the purposes of this exercise, dead and a loser, Hawk felt satisfied. If nothing else at least he'd taken one of them out with him. When he looked closer and saw it was Pretty Boy, he felt even better.

"Game over." Hawk smiled at the surprised and paint-splattered Dalton.

Barely a beat passed before Dalton nodded. "Yes, it is, Hawkins. Matt, make sure Hawkins has those orders for his special assignment waiting for him when he gets back to the garrison."

Pretty Boy flashed his pearly whites at him.

Hawk had temporarily forgotten about that damn special assignment. He stifled a groan.

Shit.

Chapter Four

Emily walked into the office and found Katie cradling the receiver and practically cooing into the phone. There was no doubt in her mind who was on the other end of that call. People in love could be so annoying. Cute, but annoying.

As she sat at her desk and proceeded to boot up her laptop, Emily noticed that even though Katie continued her conversation with BB, at least her boss had the decency to quit the lovey-dovey stuff in deference to the lack of privacy.

"I told Em about the baby. Mmm, you're right. It probably is smartest to start transferring a few things sooner rather than later. I will, I swear."

Unashamedly, Emily listened to the half of the conversation she could hear. After all, her name had been mentioned. That made it okay. Right?

The printer across her and Katie's shared office began to buzz and spew out a few pages. The part of Emily's brain that wasn't eavesdropping found that odd. Katie's computer wasn't even turned on and Emily had yet to open any files, let alone print them. But she was too intrigued by what Katie and BB would be transferring sooner rather than later to worry much about the printer.

Were BB and Katie moving so they could be together full time? And if so, where? More importantly, what did that mean for Emily and her job here in New York?

"It's here. Tell him I got it." The phone conversation continued. "Have fun going out tonight and safe flight home, baby, in case I don't get to talk to you before you leave. I love you too. Bye."

Emily noticed the tears in Katie's eyes as she hung up the phone. "You okay?"

Katie glanced up. "I'm fine. It's just the hormones. I can't even say goodbye without crying over it. Someone should really warn women that being pregnant also makes you insane."

Emily laughed. "I'll keep that in mind." Then she couldn't wait any longer to ask the question uppermost in her mind. "What are you going to do? I mean, where will you live once the baby is born and you get married? Down south near the base for his job, or here in New York so you can keep working? Or are you going to keep up the long-distance thing?"

Katie shook her head. "With the baby, a long-distance relationship would be ridiculous. But I can't expect him to give up his career for me."

"And he would never ask you to give up your career for him," Emily added.

"Exactly." Katie nodded.

Knowing her boss the workaholic would probably shrivel up and die if she wasn't able to work anymore, Emily could appreciate Katie's difficult decision. Of course, motherhood could change things.

"So what then?" Emily asked.

"Well, I kind of have a plan for that. It seems like we've picked up a lot of business in the south, especially with the latest military-recruitment ad campaigns. I'm thinking about suggesting opening a southeast branch. I could still fly to New York whenever necessary, but home base would be down south."

Emily hesitated before nodding. "Okay. I can do the south. My hair will frizz, but otherwise I won't miss the New York cold winters, or the outrageously expensive rent and super-sized cockroaches."

Katie smiled. "Thanks, Emily, but don't start packing yet. If I'm able to go full term with the baby, if the bosses agree to this and if I move—so many ifs—but if this all ends up happening, you don't have to follow me, you know. You can stay here in New York and continue to work."

"You don't want me to come with you?" Surprise and hurt colored Emily's voice.

"Of course I want you with me. I'd be lost without you. But you're getting too experienced for the job of my assistant. You need to start taking on clients of your own. The day will come when you will be able to totally replace me, I'm sure."

Emily had been solely responsible for organizing absolutely every minute of Katie's daily life and holding down the fort at the office while she was away on her many business trips or visiting BB. Katie was so focused on work she would probably forget to eat if BB or Emily didn't remind her. That concern kept Emily pretty busy.

In addition, Emily was sometimes responsible for handling the talent—fetching non-fat lattes or bottled sparkling imported water for the models they dealt with for their marketing firm. But that was about it.

Thinking about all the clients, bosses, divas, bitches, queens and crap that Katie dealt with daily, Emily cringed at the thought of taking it all on herself. "I'm not sure I'm qualified to totally replace you quite yet."

"Oh, you're qualified. You better be, because I'm about to give you your very first big solo assignment."

Big solo assignment?

Emily peered at Katie to confirm she'd heard correctly. "You're giving me a solo assignment?"

Katie grinned and nodded. "Mmm, hmm. It was initially BB's idea actually. He's worried about my working too hard when I travel. But I'm in total agreement with his suggestion on this one."

Travel? *Yay!*

Fears of divas and queens forgotten, Emily sat up a little straighter now. "For real? You'd trust me all alone with a client?"

Katie shook her head. "Why in the world are you so surprised?"

Emily opened her eyes wide. "Uh, because you're a control freak, for one thing."

Katie's mouth screwed up at the truth of that statement. "Maybe I was a little bit before."

"You think?" Emily couldn't help the sarcasm.

"Hey. Do you want this assignment or not?" She raised one perfectly shaped auburn brow in warning.

"Yes. And I'm sorry. You are the perfect boss, control issues and all." Emily pasted on an overly sweet smile.

"Well, I am also a pregnant control freak and I'm thinking a trip to Germany, if not Afghanistan, isn't the best idea right now."

"Germany or Afghanistan?" Emily had to wonder what this assignment was.

42

Katie nodded in response.

Emily let out a breath. "All right. That's okay. I like travel. I'm ready for anything, Katie." Maybe not quite ready for Afghanistan, but she'd worry about that later.

Katie laughed while shuffling through a pile of papers and file folders on her desk. "I certainly hope you are ready, because I'm afraid it might not be easy."

God, Emily hoped she wouldn't be stuck working with some German-speaking model on this assignment. She could get by with a few words of French, even Italian, but German?

"Ah ha." Katie must have found whatever she had been looking for. "Here you go."

Emily's eyes opened wide as her boss thrust a file into her hands.

"US Army Marketing Campaign." Emily read the label aloud. An uncontrollable smile spread across her face as visions of soldiers danced in her head.

"Yes, but I'm not exactly sure you should be so happy about it." There was concern in Katie's tone.

"Why not? You met and fell in love with BB during the Special Ops Recruitment Ad Campaign."

Katie nodded. "Yes. That I did."

"And we'll be using an actual Army guy for the shoots, just like we used BB because he was a real Special Operative for the last one?"

"Yes."

The joy nearly bubbled out of Emily. She tried but didn't quite control the squeal of happiness that escaped her lips. No diva, queen models of either sex for her first real assignment. Nope. She was getting to work with a real man. One of Uncle

Sam's finest of her very own. Emily was more than ready for that.

Maybe she would get to pick the guy. Emily imagined a long line of uniform-bedecked soldiers, dog tags jingling as they all waited to meet her approval. Having to meet dozens, maybe hundreds of men had to put the odds in her favor.

The thought of stumbling upon fairytale love, the kind Katie and BB had found, had her smiling even broader…until Katie's insistent head-shaking ruined her good thoughts.

"What?" Emily sounded whiny, but she hated having her fantasy ruined, especially by a woman who already had her own hero cast.

"I just don't think you should be daydreaming about this particular soldier."

This particular soldier? Disappointment warred with anticipation within her. "You've already picked him?"

"Not me personally, but yes, he's been chosen."

Was that a smirk on Katie's face?

"Who chose him?" And he had better be right, not only for the ad campaign but also for her. And single. God, she hoped he wasn't married.

"BB picked him for us."

Emily considered Katie's answer a moment.

Former underwear model turned Special Operative turned military-recruiting poster boy, BB Dalton was so good looking he bordered on beautiful. He must know some handsome guys in the military, right? Did really hot guys hang out together in packs the way gorgeous female models did?

In any case, being a former model himself, BB would know the importance of having the right look for the ad campaign. The model had to be attractive.

"Okay." Emily nodded slowly, still wondering why Katie was hesitant about this candidate.

It would all work out just fine. BB was the sweetest man on earth. The perfect gentleman. No way would he pick a jerk for Katie and Emily to work with. The happiness bubble returned.

Emily flipped open the folder and shuffled through the few papers inside. "Is there a picture in here?"

"Not in the client folder, no. The model was a...uh...recent decision. Actually, I'm not considering it's a done deal yet. BB said he is one hundred percent sure he'll be the one, but the guy hasn't even received the info for the assignment yet. He'll get it when he gets back to his garrison tomorrow. Until he gets the orders, I'm not convinced he won't back out." Katie shrugged. "We'll know for sure soon, I guess."

Emily pouted, the nearly useless file in her hand. "So there is no information on him at all?"

Katie smiled. "Relax. Check the printer."

"The printer?"

"Matt, BB's computer-genius friend, sent a few background documents directly to our printer."

"How the heck...?"

Katie shook her head. "Honestly, I don't know how he did it. Quite frankly, I think I don't want to know how Matt hacked into our wireless network from Europe and sent a document directly to our printer."

Emily glanced at the printer. Katie was probably right. Some things were better left unasked.

"I think there might be a picture of our potential model there," Katie continued.

That sent Emily flying across the room. She skidded to a stop and grabbed the pages waiting for her there in the printer tray.

She flipped through. "Damn. There's no picture, but there is a spec sheet. Staff Sergeant David Hawkins."

Mmm. That was a nice name. Emily Hawkins. Emily Price Hawkins. Staff Sergeant and Mrs. David Hawkins.

She continued reading. "He's thirty years old and seventy-two inches tall. That's..."

Emily squinted at the ceiling, doing the math until Katie interrupted her effort. "Six feet."

Excellent. Emily liked tall men. He'd look nice next to her five-foot-five-inch frame even if she wore heels.

"Hazel eyes. That's good. If we put him in Army green, it will bring out any green tint in his eyes for the photos." Her head spun with the possibilities.

"Really, Em. I don't think you should expect too much."

Emily frowned at Katie. "What aren't you telling me?"

The big sigh her boss released, accompanied by her guilty look, did not bode well.

"Emily, the soldier selected may not exactly be happy about this assignment."

"Is that all? You told me BB wasn't happy when he was ordered to do the recruitment campaign either, and that worked out fine."

More than fine. Katie had never been happier since meeting BB.

Nope. Emily was not about to cancel her dreams of happiness over one disgruntled soldier pouting over a few photo shoots. She'd win him over fast enough and prove to Katie she could handle a big, supposedly difficult, assignment all on her own.

Big. Mmm. Most likely her soldier was big and muscular, as well as tall and handsome. This day was turning out pretty great and it was still only morning.

"I just wish there was a picture." Pouting, she looked accusingly at the printer...and noticed the blinking red light. The machine was out of paper.

"Oh my God. There are more pages." Flying into action, Emily nearly ripped off one short, pale pink-polished fingernail tearing into a fresh ream of paper. She loaded it into the printer tray.

Tapping her foot while Katie laughed at her across the room, Emily waited impatiently for the next page to print.

"Come on, come on." She watched the printer, which was obviously not listening to her judging by how slowly it chugged along. Emily glanced up at her boss with frustration. "This is taking forever. We need a new printer."

Katie smiled indulgently but did get up to walk over and wait with Emily.

Finally, a color photo emerged ever so slowly from the machine. Close-shorn dark hair appeared first, followed by serious, piercing eyes. There was a strong, square chin and then a chest so broad and forearms so thick they could have easily belonged to a lumberjack.

David Hawkins's features would never be considered perfect like BB's. Instead, he was ruggedly handsome and all manly man. BB had chosen the quintessential warrior to represent the US Army.

Emily started grinning before the printing finished. Eyes never leaving the photo, she asked, "When do I meet him?"

Chapter Five

First was the humiliation of having to hike down the mountain alongside Task Force Zeta as they relived each and every kill among themselves. Sometimes they even stopped to enlighten Hawk and his men as to what Hawk's squad had done wrong during the mock slaughter.

Then Hawk had the pleasure of having to, while still wearing the game-ending paintball stain on his back, meet with Commander Miller once again back at the base camp. Miller had apparently watched and listened to every step of his golden boys' victory courtesy of Matt Call-Me-Computer-God Coleman.

Now—the topper at the end of one hell of a shitty day— having drinks with Zeta. It was an invitation from Miller that Hawk thought best not to refuse even though the dead last thing he wanted to do was bond with frigging Task Force Zeta and discuss the exercise. At least they'd gotten to eat some chow first. Hawk definitely could not have faced this on an empty stomach.

"Losing is more important than winning, if you learn from your mistakes." Jimmy Gordon delivered that advice in a southern drawl so thick Pennsylvania-born Hawk nearly needed a translator to interpret for him.

"Come on. We'll go over with you exactly what you did wrong." Gordon had the nerve to make that offer while smiling and truly looking like he meant every frigging friendly word.

Hawk didn't want to talk to any one of them, but the beer at the pub was German, dark and strong, and the pool table actually had all of its balls. All in all, since they couldn't fly out until morning, this might not be such a bad way to spend an evening, if he didn't have to sit here and listen to Zeta recap what he and his men had done wrong.

They didn't do anything fucking wrong. He wanted to shout that at them. They were outmaneuvered by technology, nothing more. That sucked, but worse, it scared the shit out of him.

"Hawkins?"

Leaning against the pool table, sighting his next shot, Hawk didn't even look up at Miller when he bit out a most likely less-than-polite, "What?"

Hawk finally glanced up in time to see the training commander's smirk. "Nothing. Just you're about to sink a striped ball."

"Yeah, so?"

Miller raised a brow. "So, you're solids, not stripes."

Shit. With a deep sigh, Hawk stepped back from the table, planted the cue stick on the ground and hung his head.

"What's wrong, son?"

The last thing he wanted to do was admit to Miller what he was about to, but he was a real man and so he would face reality.

"That loss to Zeta today shook my confidence, sir. I mean, when I said I wanted Zeta to play full out I didn't realize what that meant. The implants, the computers...we're not ready, sir."

He looked at Miller and told him, with as much conviction as he could put into his voice, the absolute truth.

"We're not ready for Afghanistan. If the insurgents come at us with anything like Zeta did today..." Hawk shook his head and continued his confession. "What if I can't bring them home alive? What happens when all that red in the snow isn't paintballs but our blood? What if my men fall in those mountains in Afghanistan just like they all fell to Zeta today?"

"They won't." Miller spoke with a confidence Hawk could only wish he felt.

"But—"

"No but about it. Do you really think the Taliban has access to the kind of training and equipment our teams have?" Miller asked.

"They might."

"They don't."

"How do you know?"

"It's my job to know. And besides that, we've faced them, right there in their own backyard. I can't tell you much more except that our teams aren't always focused on training, son. A few years ago, I led Zeta personally into those exact mountains where you're headed and beyond them, and I brought them all back out again. Alive. And if you repeat what I just told you, I'll deny every word."

Hawk couldn't care less that Miller and his SpecOps had sometime in the past most likely trespassed in a country they shouldn't have been in. He was more worried about his guys and keeping them alive. But at least now the close, easy camaraderie between Miller and Zeta made more sense. They'd been together for a long time and they'd been through things he likely couldn't even imagine.

50

"No disrespect, sir, but with those men and that equipment I'm not surprised you and Zeta all came out alive. Unfortunately I've only got my normal, human men and crap for equipment."

"First, the guys on Zeta are regular men just like you. When you stop wallowing and get to know them better, you'll find that out."

When Miller chastised, he pulled no punches. Hawk bit his tongue to keep himself silent after the wallowing comment, true though it may be.

"Second, I can tell you this about what you're walking into in Afghanistan." Miller continued undeterred. "The remaining Taliban factions survive only because of a thriving drug trade. If they were based anywhere else besides in the largest poppy-producing region in the world, they'd have little to no funding and be totally screwed.

"I'll concede that works in their favor. However, they're also in a region in constant turmoil. It's occupied by foreign powers but ruled by a newly created government as well as, unofficially, by the local warlords and tribal elders. Having too many heads like that leads to confusion and anarchy. Sometimes that climate will help the insurgents get a rare but small victory, but ultimately it leads to their defeat."

"How?" Hawk frowned. Those sounded like the perfect conditions for the bad guys to thrive.

"Their own allies turn on them, when they're not turning on each other. Most of the Taliban is living in squalor and chaos in those mountains. And believe me, they don't have anyone like our Matt Coleman designing their equipment."

The mention of Coleman aside, Hawk listened closely as Miller spoke. Now that he knew the man had been there, his words held more weight, though he said nothing that Hawk didn't to some degree already know.

"You and your men are good, Sergeant Hawkins. You held your own better and for far longer than I anticipated today. You'll have the advantage in those mountains. Trust me."

"Yes, sir." Hawk managed a nod, whether he believed it deep down or not.

"I've had about enough of chasing balls around a table. How about a beer?" Miller offered.

Now that was one thing Hawk could totally agree with Miller on. "Yes, sir. I'd love one."

But once Hawk was leaning against the bar, strategically placed there by Miller, he realized Miller's sudden craving for beer had nothing to do with thirst and everything to do with throwing him in the path of Zeta's *normal* guys just to prove his point.

Miller introduced him to a dude named John Blake—no rank or service branch specified, Hawk guessed these guys were above that—and then Miller disappeared.

"So you're an Army staff sergeant." Blake shook his head with a laugh.

Hawk had noticed Blake's grin when Miller had mentioned Hawk's branch and rank during the introduction. It seemed to still amuse the guy. Hawk decided he'd had about enough for today without this guy and his attitude too.

Hawk straightened his spine, his knuckles whitening around his beer. "Yeah. What about it?"

Blake shrugged. "It's just that not too long ago I was you. I was Army Staff Sergeant John Blake. I was a tank commander in Ramadi."

"Ramadi. I'd heard things were pretty bad there." With more respect for Blake, Hawk decided to give him a pass. The cold beer sliding down his throat didn't hurt his newfound generosity either.

"Bad is an understatement." Blake laughed. "We were eyeball deep in snipers at camp to the point we couldn't even eat in the chow hall without body armor. A few weeks before I left, I watched one of my men get hit with a vehicle-borne IED right in front of my eyes while he was dismounted. He was out of that tank following my orders. Good thing he's got a hard head and lived."

Blake shook his head again and took a sip of his beer. "And now look where I am and what I'm doing. I've got more shit implanted in my body than I ever knew existed, and I'm running around in the Alps playing what's probably the most expensive game of paintball on earth. What a difference a few months can make."

"You're trying to tell me a few months ago you were just a normal Joe out there in the sandbox?" Hawk frowned.

Blake nodded. "Yup. It was my third, and I guess my final tour."

"So what happened? How did they get you?"

He laughed. "You make it sound like they took me hostage and brainwashed me or something. Like an alien abduction."

Exactly. At first glance, all the Zeta guys had a bit of that Stepford-wife quality to them. Too perfect, too coordinated, too in tune with each other. As if they were humans replaced by robots, just like in that movie.

"I find it hard to believe that they pluck totally average guys out of the theater and turn them into you super soldiers."

Blake shrugged. "I can't speak for the rest of them, but in my case, yeah, believe it."

"So you're honestly trying to tell me you're all regular guys, just like me, but with better toys?"

At that, Blake laughed out loud. "Yeah, they...we...do have some pretty amazing toys, half of which Coleman over there invented. Now, he is not normal. He's an honest-to-goodness card-carrying genius."

When Hawk still wasn't convinced, Blake continued. "Look, I'm not saying any one of the troops out there would be right for the teams. Of course they're more selective than that. You have to have excellent basic skills as well as certain qualities. The ability to work in a group or alone. The aptitude to both lead or follow, and to switch between the two on a moment's notice."

"And that's it?"

"Well, no. It helps to be a language expert like Trey Williams over there. Or be able to drop a man with your bare hands like Jack Gordon. Or never miss a shot like Jack's brother, Jimmy Gordon. Or be a bomb expert like Bull Ford, or a diving and swimming champion like BB Dalton."

Yeah, Hawk got the idea. All perfectly regular guys. Sure. He snorted out a laugh.

"Okay, yeah, a lot of the guys used to be what you'd consider elite. Rangers. Delta Force. BB was a SEAL. But not me. I was just a tanker." Blake shrugged.

"So then why you? They all have specialties. What's yours?"

Blake smiled. "I asked Miller that exact question when he mysteriously showed up at camp in Ramadi one day. He made quite an impression, I can tell you that, dressed head to toe in his black body armor."

"And?"

"He said I had an instinct. Some innate ability to think like the bad guys, and that was as valuable a skill as any of the others." Blake shrugged again as if he had trouble believing it himself.

"I've been told I have that instinct in me." Hawk wasn't one to brag, but both superiors and guys he'd served with had said that about him.

Staying one step ahead of the baddies was a skill that had kept him and his men alive more than once. Or perhaps it was just dumb luck. At this point, Hawk wasn't so sure anymore.

Blake nodded. "I know you do. I saw it today during the exercise."

Hawk let out a bitter laugh. "You mean the slaughter."

"It's all in the toys, Hawkins. Just the toys." Blake smiled and raised his beer to salute Hawk.

Against his will, Hawkins smiled along with him. But God help him if Miller was wrong and the bad guys got their hands on those toys too.

He was still smiling when Dalton appeared at his side. "So, Hawkins. Your assignment is all set and approved."

That information chased the short-lived humor right out of him.

Blake, looking amused, turned to Dalton. "You're really going to make him go through with that?"

Pretty Boy bobbed his head. "Damn right, I am. A bet is a bet. It's all set up and ready to go."

Hawk glared at Blake. "You know what this is about?"

"Oh, yeah. He wanted me to do it originally, but apparently I'm not right for it now that I'm no longer enlisted Army. Not that I was going to do that shit anyway."

"If the commander told you to do it, Blake, you'd do it. Believe me. How do you think I got roped into it last year? The commander ordered me."

55

Hawk had the sudden urge to rip his own hair out of his head. "What is this *it* you're both talking about? Come on, Dalton. I lost. I admit that. I'll take the stupid assignment, but you at least have to tell me what it is."

"The orders will be waiting for you back at Hohenfels." Pretty Boy said it with a warning glance at Blake. The look said he better not spill the beans in the meantime.

Why was everyone being so mysterious?

"Hey, Hawkins? You got a girl?" A new voice coming from somewhere behind Dalton asked.

What the hell did his love life have to do with anything, and who the fuck was asking? Leaning past Dalton so he could identify the speaker as the computer god himself, Hawk frowned. "No. Why?"

"Because after this assignment, you will." Matt Coleman joined their conversation uninvited. "Maybe too many of them. Not too long ago, the team had to physically protect BB here from his adoring female fans at a bar. Of course, that wasn't such a chore. Especially the one who took her shirt off so he could sign her tits."

Fans? Adoring female fans ripping their clothes off? Hawk glanced at Blake, who shrugged. "Don't look at me. That was before my time."

"So anyway, Hawkins, I wanted to say good job today." The computer god actually sounded sincere.

Reminded again of the loss, and that Matt Coleman and his computers were the cause of it, Hawk scowled. "Yeah, thanks."

"No, really. I mean it. If I didn't have your entire squad mapped with thermal satellite images so I was able to tell our boys your exact locations, you might have had a chance."

Thermal satellite images. Crap. The word *cheaters* sprang to Hawk's mind again as he let out a disgusted sigh before taking another gulp of his beer.

"Toys, Hawkins. Just toys." Blake grinned once again.

Hawk was starting to really hate these boys and their toys.

Chapter Six

On the flight to Germany, Emily read and reread every document in the file Katie had given her—the plans and goals for the marketing campaign and, more importantly, the information about David *Hawk* Hawkins. BB had supplied them with the soldier's nickname, but there was scarce little else she knew about him. What there was, she devoured eagerly.

Too excited to really concentrate on anything, Emily totally ignored both the paperback novel she'd bought at the airport shop and Jai Devereaux, the photographer on the assignment with her. Out of guilt, Emily finally turned the book over to Jai to read on the long, boring overseas flight.

When Katie had rushed to schedule phase one of the campaign, the photo shoot, for as soon as possible, Emily hadn't argued. For some reason, Katie was convinced Hawk would back out and they'd have to find a replacement.

Emily's motives for the rush were very different.

She'd scrambled to secure both a photographer and plane tickets and had done so incredibly fast. Just days after BB had chosen Hawk, Emily was in the air and on the way to meet him in Germany.

Hawk. God, she loved that nickname. It was so manly. She glanced down at the file for the thousandth time. Staff Sergeant David S. Hawkins. Aka Hawk.

Oh, yes. A man with a name like that brought to mind all sorts of images and possibilities, and Emily considered each and every one of them repeatedly throughout the flight. And during the wait for the luggage. And on the drive to the base at Hohenfels, where she hoped her dreams would finally come true.

"How long until we get there?" It was the second time during the drive from the airport she'd asked that question, but she couldn't help herself. She was as excited as a kid on Christmas morning.

Behind the wheel of the rental car, Jai raised one dark eyebrow and glanced at her sideways. "Anxious to get there, are we?"

She may have known Jai for two years now and worked with him on countless of Katie's marketing campaigns, but that didn't mean she told him everything. No way was she willing to divulge her true hopes for this shoot—the real reason her hand shook as she held the file she'd once again taken out.

Prince Charming was just miles, or rather kilometers, away now. And after studying him on paper for days, Emily was already half in love with him.

"Of course I'm anxious. This is the first solo assignment Katie's ever trusted me with."

"Yeah, about that. How did you get her to do that? She's usually totally hands on."

"Don't you mean a control freak?"

Jai's dark face broke into a grin. "Yeah. So what happened?"

Emily bit her tongue about the pregnancy. That wasn't her news to tell, so she shrugged. "I guess she thinks I'm ready."

She hoped her boss was right.

"You'll do fine." Jai's dreadlocks swung as he pivoted his head to glance at her and then turned quickly back to the road. A car right on their tail flashed its lights and then passed them in the oncoming lane of traffic.

Damn, people drove fast here in Germany. Emily was certainly glad Jai had offered to take the wheel. Once she could breathe again after the near traffic disaster, she decided to try and get some work done during the remainder of the trip. "I've got some ideas for shots."

"Great. Shoot." Jai grinned at his own little joke.

Rolling her eyes, Emily couldn't help but smile herself. "I've been considering what to have Hawk wear. I guess we have to get a few of him in his dress uniform. But I really want a bunch of pictures in those cute camouflage pants too."

"Of course. I totally agree. Camo was all over the runways in Milan and Paris this season."

"I know." Excited, it wasn't until she saw Jai's smirk that Emily realized he was teasing her.

"Sorry, Em. Couldn't resist." Jai winked in answer to her scowl. "Go on. What else did you have in mind?"

Glancing at the death grip Jai had on the steering wheel as another car honked and whizzed past, rocking both them and the vehicle, Emily decided the rest could wait. "Let's see what we find when we get there. We might get more ideas on site."

"Looks like you don't have long to wait now, because here we are."

Emily put down the folder and saw the high fence of the base coming into view. She felt her heart thud harder. No, there wasn't long to wait at all.

Jai slowed the car to a crawl as they neared the two armed, make that very armed, guards at the gate. He stopped and rolled down the window. "Jai Devereaux and Emily Price. We're here to photograph Staff Sergeant Hawkins. We're expected, I believe."

"Yes, sir. IDs, please."

"Got your passport handy?" Jai looked at Emily expectantly as he passed his own to the guard through the open window.

"Um, oh. Yeah. Hold on." Emily searched through her large and now rather unorganized carry-on and finally, after a brief moment of panic, found her passport in the side pocket. She handed it to Jai, who gave it to the scary guard for his intense scrutiny.

"I'll have to ask you both to exit the vehicle."

Panicked, Emily shot Jai a look. "What did we do? Are they going to search us?"

Oh my God. What if they strip-searched her? Was she wearing nice underwear? She couldn't remember.

"It's fine, Em. Just do as they say." Jai looked much calmer than she felt.

Emily stared at Jai, suddenly unable to move. "But—"

"Em. Trust me. Just get out of the car, please...and stop talking." Jai stared back as the armed and ready guards waited in stony silence for them to get out of the car.

Here was an unexpected wrench in Emily's fairytale scenario. Getting strip-searched or shot or thrown in a foreign prison by the guards at the gate.

The one guard who had moved to her side of the vehicle made Emily so nervous it took her two tries to get the door of the car open. When he told her to leave her bag inside, she nearly passed out from anxiety. Airport security, she was used to. Stone-faced men with machine guns calling her *ma'am* as they ordered her about and searched her belongings was quite another.

Although the sun shone brightly, Emily wrapped her arms closer around herself to ward off both the cold air and the chill of fear.

After one guard had finished inspecting the front and back seats while the other one stood by and watched with weapon in hand, the first camouflage-clad soldier turned to Jai. "Pop the trunk, sir."

While Emily decided men in camouflage uniforms might not be so sexy after all, Jai nodded and reached in to hit the button on the door. It released the latch on the trunk where they'd stowed their luggage and photographic equipment at the airport.

Just as Emily decided she was going to call Katie as soon as possible and tell her she would never take another military assignment again, a soldier rushed toward them in a light jog. Instinct had her taking a step back, until she noticed he was smiling and had his hand extended in greeting. The fact he wasn't armed with some kind of machine gun also helped calm her immensely.

"Miss Price." She shook his hand and then watched as he turned to Jai. "Mr. Devereaux. I'm Ryan Pettit. The captain sent me down to escort you."

Pettit watched as the guards replaced Jai's camera equipment carefully back in the trunk. "We send a soldier down to meet any photographers and reporters and then after a routine inspection of the equipment, we sign them in under our care."

Emily breathed for what seemed like the first time since they'd pulled up to the gate. Jai sent her a look that said, *I told you so*, but she still had no intention of apologizing to him for being worried. The entire experience had been nerve-wracking and she would definitely yell at Katie at the earliest opportunity for not warning her about base procedure.

After a short interaction with the guards that included a nod, some salutes and very few words, Pettit turned to them. "We're good to go. I can ride in the backseat and direct you where to drive."

Just having him in the car made Emily feel better. Kind of like the guards would be less likely to shoot her if one of their own was seated directly behind her in the line of fire. Pettit's smile and enthusiasm was infectious. Once out of view of the guardhouse, she began to relax.

"The captain didn't go into any detail except that you're here for a photo shoot. So what are you going to photograph?" Pettit, sitting in the center of the back bench seat so he could both give Jai directions and talk to Emily, leaned forward.

"It's a new marketing campaign to establish stronger branding for the US Army. We're hoping to raise public awareness and increase recruitment." Emily turned in her seat and recited verbatim the goals Katie had developed for the campaign.

Pettit laughed. "Okay. Whatever you say. Turn right up here."

Jai nodded and did as he was told, driving at a snail's pace, which also helped to calm Emily's nerves after the hour and a half speed-of-light drive from the airport in Munich.

"I don't know much about marketing and stuff but branding means logos and slogans and things, right?"

She nodded. "Pretty much. Yeah."

"But the Army already has that. Army slogans are classic. Be all that you can be. Army Strong. They're great. Are you going to change it all?"

"No, just reinforce it and make it stronger." Emily felt the need to reassure him since he seemed very attached to the existing slogans.

Pettit nodded. "How you going to do that? Make it stronger?"

"By giving the Army a face the people can relate to." *Hawk's face*, Emily thought. "One soldier that will represent all of you."

"Really? Cool. So who—oh wait. I missed the turn." Pettit interrupted his own question. "We'll have to turn left at this corner and then left again. It's the first building, right there on the corner. You can just park at the curb."

As soon as the car stopped, Pettit jumped out and opened Emily's door for her. Military guys were so polite. She got a tingle again in anticipation of meeting Hawk.

"I'll run in and tell the captain you're here then come back out and help you unload your equipment. Captain has a room cleared for you to set up in. You can leave your stuff there overnight if you want. It's secure."

After relaying that information, Pettit trotted off and Emily had the opportunity to consider just how sweet soldiers were...at least the ones without guns who weren't searching her.

What the hell?

Hawk stared down at the large manila envelope lying on top of the blanket on his rack. He dropped the unopened letters he'd gotten during mail call onto the bed and reached for the envelope.

The moment he opened it and pulled out the paper, he knew what it was. Orders for Dalton's damn special assignment.

Sitting down heavily, he read over the duty he'd let Pretty Boy talk him into betting. When no orders had shown up immediately upon his return from the training in the Alps, Hawk had deluded himself into thinking this mystery assignment had been Dalton's idea of a practical joke.

No such luck. Even reading it again didn't change the contents.

"No. No fucking way." He shook his head and spoke out loud in his empty quarters.

"What's up, Hawk?" Wally poked his head through the open doorway.

Hawk glanced up at Wally. "Um, nothing. Just a, um, letter from home." He lied and folded the computer printout in thirds, hoping Wally would think it was a letter even though it looked far more like orders than mail.

"Everything okay?"

"Yeah, it's just um, my sister. She's uh, dating some idiot. No big deal."

"She cute, your sister? Give her my address. We can be pen pals. I'll knock that other guy right out of her mind with my charm." Wally grinned wide.

"Yeah, right, 'cause you would be a real improvement over her dating an idiot." Lie or not, Wally the womanizer dating Hawk's sister, or even being pen pals with her, was not going to happen. At least not during Hawk's lifetime.

"Damn right, I would. Besides, chicks love me. You got a picture of her?"

"Get out of here, Wally, and let me finish reading my mail."

"Just keep me in mind." With one final grin, Wally was gone.

Thank God, because Hawk had enough to deal with right now. The moment the coast was clear of Wally and his curiosity, Hawk headed out of the barracks to find someone of some authority. His sole goal was to get out of this assignment if it killed him.

There was no way he was going to do this. No way his superiors would make him do this. Why should he have to follow orders that Dalton and Coleman had somehow finagled? After all, this wasn't a real assignment. He wouldn't be saving lives or even taking them, but instead... Hawk shuddered at the thought of what he would be doing.

Fucking Dalton. No wonder he'd looked so smug about this mystery assignment, and it made total sense that he'd already done it himself. Damn white-toothed fancy boy probably enjoyed it too.

Thinking back to his last discussion with Pretty Boy and the Zetas—as he'd come to think of them—things started to make even more sense. Coleman's mention of the female attention Hawk would garner from this assignment. Blake saying he couldn't do it because he was no longer regular Army.

Fuck. He'd walked right into this. He would never, ever agree to something without knowing all the details again.

Hawk was shaking, vibrating with anger and tension by the time he got to the Head Shed. It was affectionately called that because the company commanders hung out there. As he had hoped, he found his own captain in the Company Orderly Room.

"Sergeant Hawkins. Pleasure to see you back."

"Yes, sir. Thank you. Captain, can I, uh, speak with you for a moment?"

Ignoring his request, Hawk's company commander turned to the other captain seated next to him. "Sergeant Hawkins and his guys had a little fun in the Alps with some of Hank's boys this past week. In fact, Hank called to compliment me on how exceptionally well the squad did during the training."

Hawk's brow rose. "Hank's boys, sir?"

"Yeah. Hank Miller. He was the training commander up there with you."

"Yes, Captain. I met him. I, uh, wasn't aware... You know him, sir?" And are on a first name basis, no less. Great. Just great.

"Oh, yeah. We were deployed together once upon a time, back when he was regular Army. Then he moved on to Delta Force, and from there, onto *the teams* as he calls the boys in black."

"I wasn't aware of that, sir. That's what I wanted to talk to you about, sir, the training and the, uh, other thing." Hawk held up the folded orders in his hand, wishing his company commander would ask the other captain in the room to leave so they could have some privacy.

No such luck. His commanding officer laughed.

"Oh, yeah. The special assignment." To Hawk's great dismay, his commander turned to his neighbor again. "You won't believe this. Sergeant Hawkins here has been chosen to be the face of the modern Army for some feel-good marketing campaign. They figure by plastering his mug all over the press, everyone will get the warm and fuzzies about us and what we're doing."

"To what end?" The captain's cohort finally spoke, looking surprised.

"Increase awareness. Encourage recruitment. Enlighten folks to our efforts for stabilization and rebuilding. Supposedly they had a similar campaign for the SpecOps starring one of Hank's guys last year. Some former SEAL who had modeling experience prior to joining up, if you can believe that."

A SEAL on Hank's team with prior modeling experience. Yup, that had to be Dalton. He had been a male model? Hawk supposed he shouldn't be surprised by that. He remembered Pretty Boy's exact words. *"I've already done it, Hawkins. Believe me."* This kind of assignment was fine for Dalton, but not for Hawk. He was a real soldier.

The captain went on. "That campaign was incredibly successful for recruitment and public relations. That's what Hank said when he sold the idea to me on the phone anyway."

So the miraculous appearance of Hawk's orders hadn't been all Dalton's doing. It had been Dalton's commander, Hank Miller, helping too. At least Hawk felt a bit better that Pretty Boy and his computer god, Coleman, weren't all-powerful.

The chances of Hawk getting out of this incredibly embarrassing and ridiculous assignment were looking slim. Still, he had to try. "Sir. That's what I wanted to talk to you about. I'm not some male model. I'm a trained soldier."

"Exactly. That's why they want you. They don't want a hired head. They want a real, battle-toughened warrior."

"Forgive my asking, sir. But have you seen the guy they used for the SpecOps ads? Because I have. He's some pretty boy who looks like he belongs in those perfume ads you see on television. I look nothing like that."

"Thank God for that. I don't want some fancy boy representing my Army." The captain shrugged. "The marketing people chose you, Sergeant. I have to trust they know what they're doing."

Bullshit. Dalton had chosen him out of spite, not some marketing expert. And how that all fit together—how Dalton got to choose the new face of the Army—Hawk still wasn't sure. Not that it mattered now. All that mattered was getting out of it.

"But how am I going to do this thing when I'm downrange? I'm deploying forward with my guys in a couple of weeks."

The company commander shook his head. "Not a problem. They're already here."

Here at the garrison, here? And who exactly was here? Hawk's heart jumped. Perhaps he'd misunderstood. Before totally panicking, he decided to clarify first. "Sir? Who's already where?"

"The photographer and the marketing person. I just got word from the gate that they've arrived. I sent Sergeant Pettit down to meet them and escort them here. In fact, they should have arrived by now..."

Pettit? No, no, no, no.

How the hell was Hawk going to keep this thing a secret if Pettit knew? The teasing would be relentless. Soldiers never forgot. He'd have to live with this forever, until the day he died, which would hopefully be soon.

Upon that thought, Pettit flew through the door. "Captain. Your civilians are here, sir."

Pulling Hawk aside, Pettit whispered with a smile, "Hawk, wait until you see this marketing chick from the States. Blonde. Cute."

Great. A woman no less. Hawk got to embarrass himself and play model in front of some blonde as well as his team leader Pettit. Just perfect.

Pettit, practically bouncing in his boots, turned back to the captain. "Sir. Miss Price was telling me about the ads. Do you know who they're going to use as their model?"

Hawk's hope grew. Pettit didn't know. Maybe there was still a chance...

The captain's face broke out into a huge smile, and all hope fled. "You're standing next to him, Sergeant Pettit."

Pettit's eyes opened wide as he looked at Hawk. "You mean Sergeant Hawkins, sir?"

With a disgusted sigh, Hawk nodded. "Yeah. It's me."

"Wow. My staff sergeant is going to be the face of the Army. How cool is that?" Pettit grinned, looking totally thrilled.

Hawk stifled a groan of dismay. "Yeah, great. Real cool."

Somewhere far in the distance, Hawk imagined he heard Dalton laughing.

Chapter Seven

"Staff Sergeant Hawkins. It's a pleasure to meet you." Inside the room they'd been assigned to use, Emily stepped forward and delivered the greeting she'd settled on and rehearsed in her mind during the flight over. She smiled and tried to stop her hand from shaking as she extended it toward Hawk.

"Sergeant." Hawk folded burly Popeye-like forearms across his chest.

"Excuse me?" Emily lowered her hand.

"It's just sergeant. Sergeant Hawkins."

"But it said your rank was Staff Sergeant."

"My rank is Staff Sergeant, but you only say sergeant when addressing me."

It didn't seem like that big of a difference that he would have to correct her like that. "Oh. Sorry."

She'd tried to be friendly. He met her overtures with what amounted to thinly veiled rudeness followed by one long glance that covered her from head to toe and all the parts in between.

Feeling exposed after that look, even in her cashmere turtleneck, wide-legged wool trousers and leather boots, she couldn't resist the urge to cross her own arms over her chest.

Cat Johnson

Boy, was she glad she'd chosen pants over a skirt. She didn't need him ogling her legs too.

"I'll be photographing you today, Sergeant." Jai, apparently not going to make the same mistake at camaraderie that Emily had made, nodded from the corner as he continued to unpack the cameras and lights they'd carried in from the car.

Silent and expressionless, Hawk nodded back.

Staff Sergeant David *Hawk* Hawkins was a lot of things, and to Emily's vast and bottomless devastation, so far none of them were good. Her heart fell. It felt as if Hawk had stomped on it, and her hopes, with one slam of his very large combat boots.

He had the muscles she'd dreamed of, but along with them came a truckload of testosterone-fueled bad attitude. He seemed every inch the serious warrior his picture had hinted at, but she sensed he was also as stubborn and unyielding as a mule.

The Neanderthal before her, the Hawk himself, waited with a stone-faced expression as Jai set up the equipment. But no, maybe he wasn't as stony as he appeared. Beneath the cold, steely exterior, Emily sensed molten anger bubbling just below the surface.

Maybe his attitude was just resistance to the assignment. Katie had warned her that could be the case. In fact, Katie had been convinced Hawk would back out of it in the beginning. If he was unhappy about this, that could account for the standoffishness.

It could be partially her own fault too. She was so used to working with sensitive, artistic, metrosexual straight guys or openly gay males that she simply didn't know what to do with a real manly man when she came across one.

Perhaps that was the problem with her dating life too. Something to think about...later. Right now she had an unhappy hulk of a male to handle. If only she could get him past this.

He was handsome in a rough-and-ready kind of way. Hot actually, with dark hair cropped close to his head, deep intense eyes that gave her a view into his emotions, which was not exactly a plus at the moment, and a body so big it would definitely let a woman know she was being held.

Emily picked her heart back up off the floor where it had first been trampled by Hawk's cold reception, dusted it off and tried to salvage both this assignment and her dreams.

"So I was thinking first we can take some shots inside using the plain backdrop Jai set up. That way I can superimpose different backgrounds for various ads as needed. Then, if it's still light enough, we can move outdoors and scout some locations for exterior action shots for tomorrow's shoot." Steeling her nerves, she made direct eye contact with him.

No comment.

Emily sighed. This was not going to be easy, but nothing worth doing was. She turned to her only ally in the room. "Jai? What do you think?"

Jai looked up from the light meter in his hand. "Huh? Oh, yeah. Sounds good, Em."

Turning back to Hawk, she let her gaze roam over him the way his had traveled up and down her before. The fright from the guards a distant memory now, she was back to appreciating the benefits of a man dressed in camouflage.

"We can shoot the camouflage outfit first, since you're already wearing it." Emily noticed one dark brow cock up. She paused and waited.

"Outfit?" Hawk scowled. "It's a uniform. An Army advanced combat uniform or ACU to be exact."

She felt her face pale at his censor. "Okay. Sorry."

This had not turned out at all the way she'd pictured in her dreams. In fact, it was becoming more and more like a nightmare.

Jai looked as if he was nearly ready, so Emily figured she'd better be brave and broach the next subject. "So we'd like to um..." how to say this without getting shot down again, "...make your, uh, physical form stand out in the photos."

There was that brow again, but this time accompanied by a smirk.

He remained silent, so she continued. "So maybe you could roll up the sleeves of your camouflage uniform shirt so we can see your arms a bit?"

Even though she'd remembered to call it a uniform and not an outfit—as if she would ever forget that again—she still got the disapproving look and head shake.

"No can do. And it's called a jacket, not a shirt."

Why couldn't he just do one little thing without being difficult as well as correcting her terminology? Humph. As if she should know what military clothes are called.

"Why can't you?" Emily widened her stance, ready for battle. He wanted to argue, she could argue.

"Because it's against the rules, that's why."

"But I swear I've seen guys with their sleeves—" The steady sway of his head still shaking at her finally stopped her in her tracks. "What?"

"You may have seen it, but it is against our regulations and I can't do it."

He meant won't do it. Emily couldn't imagine that his captain really gave a darn what his sleeves looked like.

"Maybe we can ask someone if it would be okay—"

He actually laughed at that. "No."

With a huff, she gave in.

"Fine. Are you allowed to take off your jacket?" Emily emphasized the word that he'd insisted on correcting her on. "Can you wear just your T-shirt or is that against the rules too?"

"Yes, I'm allowed."

Finally, a yes, but still he didn't move.

"Could you please take off your jacket?"

Hawk smirked boldly but thankfully complied. With a chuckle, he took it off.

Now he was laughing at her? Emily planted her hands on her hips. "What's so funny?"

"It's been a long time since a woman ordered me to take my clothes off. Maybe this gig won't be so bad after all." Hawk hung what still looked more like a shirt than a jacket on the back of a chair and turned back to her. He paused with a hand on his nylon belt. "Pants too, doll?"

Doll?

She narrowed her eyes at Hawk. "No, thanks. Maybe later."

Pig. Worst of all, a pig with bulging biceps and beautiful pecs beneath a very tight T-shirt. His dog tag chain nestled right between those delectable pecs. Emily suddenly imagined him standing before her without the shirt. All big and burly.

What was she doing? He was such a...a... There simply were no words to describe him.

The chuckle from Jai's direction didn't help Emily's mood. She shot him a nasty look as well.

Emily turned back to Hawk and sighed. She had to get into a professional mindset. No more pouting that he wasn't Prince Charming. No more bickering because he was acting like the typical difficult model. She was used to that at least.

Thinking like Katie would, Emily imagined the finished print advertising. Hawk, standing in his T-shirt and camo pants. Arms crossed...make that hairy arms crossed.

Darn. BB was practically hairless but Hawk, no such luck. What were the chances of Emily being able to get him to wax the hair off his forearms? And if they chose to do a few topless shots, would he wax his chest? Probably his back would require de-hairing, also. Stifling a laugh at the ridiculous notion, she figured the odds of him agreeing were slim to none.

Could they airbrush out that much hair? And exactly how many tattoos were the tan T-shirt and camouflage pants hiding? Now that she was getting to know him better, he seemed the type to have ink, and lots of it. Probably a really crude naked lady or obscenities. Or maybe some morbid, bloody skull tattoo. Emily could only guess. She and Katie hadn't discussed the possibility of tatts. Perhaps they could airbrush any of those out too.

Then a small detail she'd missed before hit her.

She frowned. "Your shirt. It's tan."

"Yeah, so?"

"So, shouldn't it be green? You know, Army green. No?"

"No."

"Why not?"

"Because it's the rules."

"Oh, come on. I know I've seen military men in olive-green shirts."

He nodded. "I'm sure you have. Marines wear green shirts. The Army wears tan T-shirts with the universal-camouflage pattern for our combat uniform."

She sighed again, deeper. Fighting the rules seemed useless, but she couldn't resist one last word. "Well, that tan does nothing to bring out the color of your eyes."

Hawk smiled broadly at that, looking genuinely amused, an emotion Emily had begun to doubt was in his repertoire.

"I'll make sure to point that out to my superiors. Maybe they'll consider changing the regulation uniform in deference to the color of my eyes."

Well, that was the highest amount of syllables she'd heard come out of him all at once the entire day.

Emily had a strong urge to stick her tongue out at him. He'd probably laugh at her for that too, so she didn't give him the satisfaction.

She heard Jai's shutter and looked up to see him snapping candid photos of Hawk, who went from a laughing smile at her expense, to a frown, to looking stern and kind of scary in a matter of seconds.

"That's great, Sergeant." Jai wore a grin. "Perfect. I want your whole range of expressions over the next few days."

That led to an even more comical expression of horror clearly written across Hawk's face. Had he just realized that whether he was happy about it or not, this photo shoot and this ad campaign starring him was going to happen? Difficult or not, he was stuck with them for the next few days and there was nothing he could do about it.

Now it was Emily's turn to smile.

The hellish part of a day he'd rather forget about finally done, Hawk headed for his bunk only to be waylaid by Wally at the door of their barracks.

"Hey, Hawk. We're heading out to get a few beers. We figure we'd better get it while we still can since there'll be no drinking or anything else fun where we're going. Wanna come?"

He could sure as hell use a beer about now after what he'd just been through, but he couldn't go out on a bender and get drunk tonight. He had to get up early in the morning and meet with the cute and curvy but dim-headed blonde and her smart-ass Rastafarian photographer again. Tomorrow they had to scout locations for exterior action shots and then shoot outside if the weather was good. They hadn't had enough light left to do it today.

Scouting locations and worrying about the light. Great, now he was starting to think like a frigging model.

"Nah. I'm heading to my room."

"Where the hell have you been for the past couple of hours, anyway?" Wally frowned as if he'd just noticed Hawk's extended and unexplained absence just as Pettit walked up.

Hawk shot a quick warning glance at Pettit and answered Wally's question. "Special assignment."

Pettit froze where he was. Hopefully the threats Hawk had levied against him in the captain's office that afternoon would keep Pettit's mouth shut and it would stay a *special assignment* as far as the rest of the squad was concerned.

He leveled Pettit one more stern look. His team leader, who couldn't comprehend why Hawk was so miserable about the whole modeling thing, rolled his eyes behind Wally's back.

"Yeah, but what kind of special assignment?" Wally continued relentlessly.

Hawk let out a short laugh. "The classified kind."

"Fine, whatever. We're leaving in thirty if you change your mind and decide you wanna come." Wally scowled and disappeared into his room.

Pettit slunk closer. "I don't understand why you—"

"My assignment. My choice." Hawk cut him off.

His team leader sighed. "Fine, but if you think your face can be featured in every Army ad worldwide and no one will notice, you're crazy."

"And if you think we're going to see any advertising in those mountains in Afghanistan, you're crazy. We'll be long gone by the time those ads hit, and a year from now or more, when we finally do come home, they'll have realized their mistake in using me and will have moved on to some other poster boy. Believe me." Hawk crossed his arms, certain his prediction would come true.

"For your sake, Hawk, I hope you're right." Shaking his head, Pettit turned back to his room.

Oh, Hawk would make sure he was right. He'd be so unpleasant to work with Goldilocks would ensure he'd never work on another assignment with her again. She'd go running looking for a new model. Dalton would just have to find her a new sucker for this job.

It was a damn shame too, to have to do that to her. She was a looker, if you liked the young and starry-eyed type. Hawk tended to go for the more experienced women himself. He had neither the time nor the patience for innocent types like the bubbly blonde from today who had wanted him to roll up the sleeves of his camo *outfit*.

Shaking his head with a laugh at that memory, he pivoted toward his own room to get his beauty sleep and curse Dalton for the thousandth time that day.

Apparently modeling was harder work than it seemed judging by his exhaustion. Quite simply, he was done in. Running through the Alps for two straight days had taken its toll on his body. And now his special assignment had done a real number on his brain too. It all caught up with him at once.

Sleep found him the moment his head hit his lumpy pillow.

"Take off your shirt, Hawk."

He did, and Goldilocks ran a brightly painted, long fingernail across his chest. He could feel her touch on his skin. It caused a shiver to shoot down through him. Standing on tiptoe in her mile-high stilettos to reach his ear, she breathed, "I want you. Now."

She didn't need to ask him twice.

Hawk reached down and hoisted her up. She wrapped her legs around him. Beneath her miniskirt, he cupped each gloriously round, bare ass cheek her thong exposed.

Somehow, she freed his erection from his pants. A slight shove had the thin string of her thong pushed to the side and him sliding easily into her with a groan and a shudder.

She gripped his head with two hands, kissing his face, his neck. When she reached his mouth, she slipped her tongue inside.

He could feel her, tight, wet, hot, as she slid up and down his slick length.

"Harder, Hawk." She was demanding, insatiable as the muscles deep inside her began to grip and pulse around him.

She cried out, loud, unashamed, with each of his thrusts until he lost all control and came with her.

Breathing heavily, Hawk awoke alone in his bunk. He'd been dreaming.

Hawk, who usually slept like a rock, had actually dreamed. Not a nice, normal nightmare either, like forgetting to get dressed and attending a Promotions Board meeting in his underwear or anything like that. Oh, no. Thanks to Dalton and his little modeling assignment, Hawk's slumber had been visited by images more appropriate for triple-X films than his weary brain.

The sticky mess covering the spent erection in his boxer briefs was a much-too-real reminder of his shame. But that was nothing compared to the knowledge that in mere hours he'd have to look Goldilocks in the eye and try not to remember how amazing it felt to fuck her, even if it had been only in his dreams.

Yeah, the way the two of them got along like oil and water, that was pretty much what she'd tell him should he ever suggest them hooking up. In his dreams.

Shit. Hawk rose from his bed and headed to the bathroom to clean up. He needed to get laid for real and soon.

Chapter Eight

Emily stirred real cream into her to-go coffee cup thinking how much she loved Europeans. No skim milk for these folks, unlike skinny-conscious Americans. In the dim light of dawn, she watched the people bustling past the window. She and Jai had met to grab coffee before heading back to Hohenfels to meet Hawk. The town nearest the US Army garrison had some surprisingly good coffee shops and restaurants.

Emily realized she was finally getting some of the military-speak down. She even knew what a garrison was now, and her uniform knowledge had been greatly increased after yesterday's photo session with Hawk. She tried not to think about that.

The best part of yesterday had been at the end of the day when they'd gotten away from the garrison and Hawk's bad mood.

Emily and Jai had found a great spot to eat out after that. They'd had a quick but sumptuous dinner before, jetlagged, they crashed early. The hotel wasn't bad either. Too bad she'd barely slept.

"Why did we decide to meet so early?" She tried not to sound too whiny then smothered a yawn.

"Because the Army starts their day early. And because we need to set up the shots and be ready to go when and if the sun finally comes out today." Jai looked up at the overcast sky darkening the pink-tinged sunrise. "I hope it doesn't snow."

So did Emily. It was bad enough that, though exhausted, she needed to be on her toes to handle Hawk. The last thing she wanted to deal with was snow during their outdoor shots. She had on her good leather boots and she hated snow...and cold and early mornings, no matter what time zone they happened to be in.

Sunrise. Honestly, she couldn't remember the last time she'd seen one of those.

Tired, dreading the day ahead and feeling a need for sugar as well as caffeine, Emily grabbed some sort of rich-looking German pastry and added it to their two coffees on the counter.

She yawned again and got out her wallet to pay. After a brief exchange with the thankfully English-speaking clerk, they left the warm shop for the frigid walk to their rental car.

Jai frowned at her as he turned the key in the ignition and waited for the car to warm for a minute before throwing it into drive. "Why are you so tired? We turned in at like seven o'clock local time. You should have had plenty of sleep."

"I didn't sleep well." She hoped Jai would leave it at that and not question her further as to why.

Not sleeping well was an understatement for last night's torture. Emily had gotten back to her room after dinner and called Katie's office line to leave a message. She'd had to lie on the voicemail and tell Katie that everything with Hawk was going perfectly. That she could handle him no problem. Then she'd fallen into bed, only to be tortured with more thoughts of Hawk as she relived each and every word exchanged between them.

That's probably what led to her dreaming about him. She hoped that was it anyway. Whatever the reason, dream she did.

It started with a photo shoot, which was understandable considering they'd had one that day. However, the model was BB and Katie was there. To her horror, Katie had begun to take BB's uniform off until he was nearly naked, then they'd started kissing each other as she watched.

Emily cringed even now at the thought. In her dream, she'd tried to look away but couldn't. Then something even more disturbing had happened. BB had morphed into Hawk, and the woman the mostly nude Hawk was making out with was suddenly no longer Katie, but Emily.

Her hands had been all over those big muscles of his as she stroked up and down his torso. It was so realistic she could feel the warmth of his skin, the hardness of his bulging biceps, the tickle of the hair on his chest against her palms. All while he'd made love to her mouth with his tongue.

She'd woken up totally freaked out and a little bit aroused. That had been it for sleep for the night. Her brain spinning and her body clock messed up from the time difference, Emily had given up on bed and taken out her laptop.

Jai had downloaded the day's shots to her computer so she'd spent the rest of the time until she'd had to get ready to meet Jai working. She'd taken Hawk's photos and played with the layout for some potential print ads.

Working with the pictures of him had done nothing to dispel the memories of that dream, but at least the work she'd done in the wee hours was a good non-sexual excuse to explain her lack of sleep to Jai.

"I woke up really early so I mocked up a few ads. I'll show them to you when we get there." She was happy to steer the discussion back to business.

"How do you think they look? Do you have all you'll need for the interior shots and close-ups?"

Emily had to admit, she was pleased with what she'd had to work with and what she'd come up with. Of course, telling Hawk he made a great model would never come out of her mouth except maybe under extreme torture.

"I think so. Although, since he's so far away..." *and such a pain in the ass,* "...we may want to take some extras. And I never did get him into his dress uniform yesterday."

Or out of it, except in her dream...

"Mmm. Right. Make sure I'm in the room when you ask him to put his dress outfit on. That should be fun." Jai grinned.

Emily scowled. So much for her supposed ally.

Hawk stood by the window and watched Goldilocks and Rasta-photographer park in front of the Head Shed and get out of their car. Surrounding him, on nearly every available surface, was all the photographic equipment from the photo session he'd been forced to partake in yesterday.

Today, he'd have to do it all again, under the direction of the blonde who'd had him coming in his sleep like a teenaged boy.

He studied her more closely today than he had yesterday when he'd dismissed her as a young, silly-though-cute annoyance. This morning, watching her juggle a large briefcase and an extra-large cup of coffee as she walked down the path from the car, he realized his nocturnal imaginings had given her a slutty sort of makeover. She didn't wear fuck-me high-heel shoes or butt-bearing mini-skirts and her nails weren't long, red talons at all.

Cocking his head to one side, he wondered why his brain would do that, because the blonde before him—nose pink from the cold, unruly curls tousled by the wind, all bundled up in her thick wool sweater and looking like the girl next door, was pretty damn cute in her own right.

He moved to the open doorway of the room, where he had a view of the main entrance of the building, just in time to see her push through the front door along with a burst of wind.

Goldilocks finally looked up and noticed him watching her.

"Morning." She met his gaze, mumbled the greeting and then looked away.

She made an obvious effort to not walk too closely to him as she passed him in the doorway. She seemed to be concentrating overly hard on setting her briefcase on one of the tables, all while not looking at him.

If Hawk wasn't mistaken, she was avoiding eye contact as she set up her laptop. Had he been such a beast yesterday that she couldn't even look at him today? Thinking about it, he realized the answer was most likely yes, and that made him feel pretty shitty.

The new face of the Army, like it or not, and he was portraying himself as an ass. Probably not the best idea since performing even this bullshit assignment badly could negatively affect his chances at a promotion.

Smiling, Rasta-man's greeting was quite a bit more welcoming than Goldie's. "Morning, Sergeant. Have you heard the weather forecast for today? All I could get on the television in the room was in German."

Predicting the weather here in winter was a no brainer. "Cold," Hawk answered simply.

Unwinding an incredibly long and multi-colored scarf from around his neck and dreadlocks, Rasta grinned. "Yeah, I'd gathered that already. But what about snow?"

The answer to that he had actually heard from one of the guys at chow. "No snow."

Rasta grinned. "Good. See, Em. Nothing to worry about." He turned toward Hawk. "City girl here reacts badly to snow."

Goldilocks, aka Em, glanced at her photographer as if she wanted to take Rasta's scarf and strangle him with it.

"Will you be okay if we do shots outdoors today in this cold?"

Hawk raised a brow at Rasta's question, remembering his recent fun in the four-foot-deep drifts in the Alps. "Don't worry about me. You should probably worry about her though."

"I'll be fine, thank you." She raised one blonde brow and shot Hawk a less-than-friendly look then turned back to her laptop screen. "Jai, can you take a look at the ad mock-ups so we know what more we need to get today?"

Very pointedly, she'd moved the subject away from her and onto the job.

"You mean besides the dress...uniform?" Rasta-man laughed as he walked toward a pissed-looking Goldilocks.

Hawk's ears perked up, not about the dress uniform part, but about Goldie having the ads done already. She moved fast. He'd assumed these frigging embarrassing photos wouldn't hit until well after next week when he was safely gone, but maybe he'd been wrong.

Trying to not look overly interested, Hawk used all of his vast skill and prowess learned over multiple tours of duty and sidled stealthily behind the two bent heads at the laptop. Glancing past Rasta-man's dreadlocks, he caught a glimpse of a portion of an ad. His ad. That was his eye glaring back at him off the screen.

Damn, no wonder Goldie wouldn't look at him today. He did look kind of scary in that one.

Goldie turned in her seat, glimpsed his face and let out a frustrated huff of air. "You don't like it."

It hadn't sounded like a question, but rather a resignation-filled statement of fact.

"I didn't say that," Hawk defended.

"You didn't have to. You're frowning."

"No, I'm not." Hawk consciously smoothed his brow muscles.

Goldie turned back to the screen, but he thought he heard a mumble sounding like, "Yeah, right."

With the click of her short pink nails against the keyboard, the picture on screen changed to another one.

The two marketing gurus were discussing some fine points of demographics and target markets or something and didn't even notice him until Hawk readjusted his stance to try and see around them, which caught Rasta's attention.

"Hey, man. Sorry. I'm in your way. I'm sure you wanna see." Moving aside, Hawk got his first full glimpse of himself.

He heard Goldie sigh. "I'm sure you hate this one too."

Hawk considered the photo before him on screen for another second. Legs planted wide, he stood wearing his T-shirt and camouflage pants with his arms crossed in front of his chest. His jaw set firm, there was no smile on his lips. His nose showed and part of his eye, but that was it. She'd cropped the photo so you couldn't see the rest of his face or even identify it as him. He loved it.

Realizing he stood in that same pose now, Hawk had to admit, Goldie and Rasta had really captured his essence.

Hawk decided to throw Goldie a bone for her efforts. "I like it."

Visibly taken aback by the compliment, Goldie shook her head slightly as if she hadn't heard him correctly. "You like it?"

"Mmm, hmm. You cut off half of my face. I like it."

Couldn't have her getting too cocky, now could he? At least Rasta-man seemed to appreciate Hawk's sense of humor. He broke out laughing while Goldie's face twisted into an angry frown.

"I agree. Not seeing your face is preferable. Perhaps I'll crop them all like that." Insult delivered, she spun back to the laptop.

"You do that, doll, and I'll owe you a big kiss plus some."

Goldie emitted something resembling a snort.

He smiled. She was sure fun to play with. In fact, reevaluating his former opinion of Goldie, Hawk decided he wouldn't mind at all playing with her some more. In all sorts of ways.

Still chuckling, Rasta moved across the room to fiddle with some of his camera equipment. "Em, I think we're good on indoor shots for now."

"What about the dress-uniform ones?" Goldie shot Hawk a look. "Are you going to have any problems with us shooting you in your dress uniform?"

"As long as you don't use real bullets. No. No problem. Shoot away."

Hawk smiled as she rolled her eyes at his corny joke. He was pretty certain using real bullets had crossed her mind at one point that morning.

"Interior shots we can take anytime using the lights, Em. I'm anxious to get outdoors and scout some locations for the

Cat Johnson

exterior shots while the weather is still good." Rasta-man
glanced up from packing a bag full of stuff, most of which Hawk
wouldn't have been able to identify the use of. Then again, it
wasn't his job to know photography equipment. It was his job to
know his garrison.

Hawk really, really did not want to be helpful for this thing
he was being forced to do. But against his will, his brain went
into overdrive and he actually had an idea for the outdoor
shoot. Rasta would love it and take a hundred more photos of
him because of it, but Hawk knew he was going to share his
idea anyway. Though it had crossed his mind at one point to let
them flounder on their own.

Oh, well. "I had some thoughts about the outdoor shots."

Looking amused, Goldie turned to him. "Really? You? Had
thoughts?"

Hawk raised one brow and rose to the challenge. "Yeah, I
do that occasionally. Think. Be real nice to me, Goldilocks, and
I might share some of my more interesting thoughts with you
sometime. I guarantee you'll enjoy it."

His pet name for her went over like a fart in a spacesuit,
judging by the expression on her face. He smiled again. Yeah,
he definitely was enjoying this verbal foreplay. But time to get
back to work so he could get this assignment over and done
with.

"Anyway, I don't know what you're looking for exactly, if
you want authentic-looking combat shots or not, but troops
come to Hohenfels for realistic force-to-force combat-maneuver
training," Hawk began.

Rasta's eyes opened wide. "So you do mission rehearsals
and stuff like that here?"

Hawk nodded. "Exactly."

"What do you use in the simulations? Lasers?"

90

Well, well. Rasta-man wasn't just a pretty face with a lot of hair. He had some sort of military experience, probably from behind the lens of his camera, but at least Hawk wouldn't have to explain everything to them both like children.

"Exactly. We have a laser-engagement system and COBs—civilians on the battlefield—who help us train. There's a village set up, totally realistic, perimeter razerwire fencing, guard towers, MPs on patrol and civilian housing where the COBs live. You'd never know you weren't in Iraq or Afghanistan."

Rasta looked excited enough to jump right out of his coffee-colored skin at that description. "And we can get permission to shoot there?"

"Captain said whatever you wanted, he'd approve. Within reason," Hawk added.

Eyes wide, Rasta began grabbing his equipment faster and stowing it in bags. "Great. Let's go."

Goldie watched him. "I guess it's all set then."

Hawk grinned. So she didn't like not being in control. Interesting and something to remember for the future.

Rasta paused and glanced at her. "Sorry, Em. Did you have an idea for something else?"

"No. I think we should trust Hawk's experience."

Goldilocks was going to trust him. He liked that idea.

Today was turning out to be pretty interesting all around.

Chapter Nine

In the dimly lit comfort of her hotel room, Emily stared into the haunting eyes of Staff Sergeant David *Hawk* Hawkins and realized her heart was not only beating faster, but parts lower were beginning to throb as well.

She reached out one finger. Running it down the screen along the side of his cheek, she shook her head at her own behavior.

Darn it. What was wrong with her libido? She should not be attracted to him. He was an unpredictable idiot. Hawk acted like a total jerk one moment, but then he came up with the perfect suggestion for their shoot the next. He'd even cooperated during it.

She'd seen a different side of him today when he'd taken her and Jai for a tour of the outdoor training village. Then more of it when, familiar, alert, capable, he'd posed for shots with huge, scary automatic weapons like they were an extension of his body.

It was a glimpse into what he must be like when he was with his men being a professional soldier instead of being a pain in her ass as a model.

The man was gorgeous to look at on the outside, and a cocky, male chauvinistic pig on the inside. And she had to admit she wanted him.

Emily leaned back from the laptop screen and the photo of Hawk decked out in his dress uniform. His chest was covered in ribbons or medals or whatever they were called. His face was stern as usual, his chin firm, his eyes piercing straight through her.

There might be more inside this man than she'd seen. Of course, that something more could be either good or bad. There was no telling for sure, but she would never know. She left for New York tomorrow.

Emily let out a sigh. She and Jai had tickets on a late-morning flight out of Germany. She was returning to work and to her boss a success with enough photos for a kick-butt ad campaign. She was also returning home without the Prince Charming she'd been so sure of finding.

A knock on the door made Emily jump nearly out of her desk chair.

"Em. You still awake in there?" Jai's voice followed the knock.

Happy she hadn't taken the time to change into her flannel pajamas, knowing Jai would tease her relentlessly for certain if she had, Emily opened the door for him.

"No, I'm not asleep. And if I had been, you sure would have woken me up."

He grinned. "But you weren't sleeping, so it's all good. And since you're awake...there's a Ratskeller right next door to the hotel. What do you say we go out and sample some of the local culture in the form of German beer and nightlife for our last night here?"

"I don't know. I thought I'd work on some more print ad mock-ups—"

"You can do that tomorrow during the flight while I sleep off a nice dark-lager hangover."

Emily laughed. No doubt that would be exactly how the flight would go.

"Okay." Then she glanced down at her wool trousers and sweater, the same ones she'd worn all day. "Am I dressed all right for a Ratskeller? I don't think I've ever been to one."

"Em, it's just a bar. You're overdressed, I'm sure. Just come on."

She'd have to trust Jai's fashion advice. She had no other choice. The rest of her wardrobe already packed in her luggage looked pretty much like what she had on but in a different color. Emily grabbed her wallet out of her briefcase and headed out.

The minute she walked into the bar she felt it, eyes on her. Lots of them, all male, and judging by the fact Hawk stood in the center of the group of males watching her, she guessed they were all soldiers from the neighboring garrison. They weren't in uniform, but they did all sport the signature military cropped hair. Two of them even walked in sync when they crossed the bar to the jukebox together.

Hawk smiled and crossed the room himself, but he wasn't following the other two. He was heading right for her. Emily took a deep breath and prepared for another verbal battle.

"Good evening, Sergeant," Jai greeted Hawk.

Hawk nodded a return greeting to Jai then he turned to her. "Hey, Goldilocks. Fancy seeing you here."

Her brows shot up, but that was all the reaction she allowed him. "Sergeant Hawkins."

Jae grinned, apparently amused at her new name, at least as far as Hawk was concerned. "Em. I'm going to get us two beers. Good with you?"

"Yeah, fine. Thanks." She scowled at her supposed friend for enjoying Hawk's teasing of her so much, but accepted his offer. Glancing back at Hawk, she had a feeling a beer, or three, would be in order tonight.

As Jai left them alone, she raised her chin. "Do you even know my name?" She confronted Hawk as he towered over her.

He grinned wider. "Yeah."

"Okay. Then what is it?" Emily crossed her arms and challenged him over the noise of the many bar patrons.

Leaning down, Hawk came so close she could feel his breath brush her ear. "It's Emily, Goldilocks."

She shivered involuntarily at the feel of his warm breath against her skin and swallowed hard, unsure what to say.

It was a simple answer to her question, though delivered in far more intimate a manner than she'd expected. She certainly never expected it to affect her as it had.

Deciding the safest course of action would be to change the subject, she did just that. "So, I looked over the shots from today. They look really great. I could email you the proofs if you wanted to see them."

Then she would have not only his email address, but also an excuse to be in contact with him after she left Germany tomorrow. Why did her heart race at that idea? He was a jerk, most of the time anyway.

Like now as he shrugged. "Whatever."

"Don't you care about the ads?"

"I have to tell you, doll. I won't waste one moment thinking about this modeling thing once the rounds start flying and the baddies start to fall."

"Fine, I won't bother you with them then."

Looking actually sincere, Hawk shook his head. "I didn't say you'd be bothering me. What I meant was I'll have a few things on my mind, like bringing the men depending on me home alive. Latest word from where we'll be in the Afghan mountains is that a storm dumped a few feet of snow and more will be on its way. And that's the good news, because at least with the snow mounds building up we actually have a perimeter defense."

"Oh." Emily didn't know much about perimeter defense, but she did hate the snow and could empathize with him about that. "Hopefully they'll get the snowplows to clean all that up before you guys get there."

Hawk laughed—a deep, rich, genuine belly laugh she'd never assumed he was capable of.

Emily frowned. "What?" Why was this guy always laughing at her expense?

Hawk could barely respond through his laughter. "Oh, Goldilocks. There aren't going to be road crews cleaning up for us."

"Isn't where you're going kind of like the set up here at Hohenfels?"

Hawk tilted his head to one side and grinned. "No, it's not."

"Oh. I figured all bases were probably the same," Emily shrugged. What did she know? It was pretty rude of him to think she should.

"No, doll. They're not, but I'm not going to a base anyway." He smiled, shaking his head. "If I was going to be at Kandahar or Bagram, then yeah, maybe we'd have some services, but not where I'll be. We literally have some dirt huts and a few rail boxes. Supplies will have to be choppered in and dropped to us. It'll be like going caveman."

Not appreciating his delight at her expense, Emily grumbled, "That should be easier for some of you than others, I suppose."

He raised one dark brow with amusement. "You calling me a caveman, doll?"

"Maybe." Emily smiled, enjoying her own cleverness.

It was the strangest thing, but bickering with Hawk kind of got her excited. Even his calling her doll was starting to sound sexy, and she hadn't even drunk the beer that Jai was now carrying her way.

Hawk, looking like he got as much pleasure from the sparring as she, grinned wide as Jai joined them.

"Sergeant, did Emily tell you? The shots we took at the training village today are awesome."

"Good, I'm glad." Strangely, Hawk looked like he meant it.

Emily grasped the topic of work before she gave in to imagining running her fingers down Hawk's massive forearm, and other things.

"I agree with Jai. The SpecOp ads Katie shot with BB were all taken in a studio. They were good but nothing like ours. The ones we took outdoors today look really authentic, like we actually shot in the war zone. As great as BB was, I think our Army ads will be even more effective because they look so real. Right down to our caveman model, here." Emily grinned and sipped her beer.

Hawk raised his glass in a salute. "Thanks. I think that may be the nicest thing you've ever said to me."

Emily laughed. "You're welcome."

"Fucking Dalton." Hawk shook his head and took another swallow from his own glass.

That got Emily's defenses up. He could pick on her, but no one picked on her boss's fiancé in front of her. "What's wrong with BB? He's practically perfect."

Hawk laughed. "If he's your perfect man, sweet thing, then I don't know what the hell you're doing hanging around with me."

Annoyed with him all over again, she stood a little straighter, but he still towered over her. "I'm not hanging around with you. You're hanging around with me. Jai and I came here tonight to absorb some local color before we leave tomorrow morning."

Jai glanced from her to Hawk and back again with a strange expression on his face. "Um, I see Sergeant Pettit over there. I think I'll go ask him...something."

Hawk grabbed Jai's arm. "Pettit knows the truth about all this, and he also knows I'll kill him if he spills the beans. But as far as the rest of them know—" he bobbed a head in the direction of the soldiers across the room standing with Pettit, "—you and she were here for the last two days taking photos of the garrison, not of me. Let's keep it that way, understood? As far as my squad is concerned, my assignment was to be your escort only. That's all. Got it?"

Jai laughed and shook his head. "Yeah, I got it. Don't worry, Sergeant."

Hawk looked more than a bit concerned as he watched Jai cross the room.

"He'll keep your secret," Emily assured him, thinking all the secrecy was stupid since his face would soon be in ads pretty much everywhere.

Hawk continued to track Jai as he joined the group of soldiers. "How long have you known him?"

"Jai? A few years, I guess. He's discreet, I promise."

He raised a brow. "You two fucking?"

"What? No." She nearly choked at the question. God, he could be so crude sometimes. "You are the rudest, biggest, nosiest..." Unable to figure out how to insult him more, she left the sentence open ended.

"And you hate how you find me attractive." He treated her to a crooked grin before sipping at his beer.

"You? Attractive? Ha!" That accusation had her sputtering. Okay, maybe she did think he was hot, but he didn't have to know that. "Don't flatter yourself. You're a job. Nothing more."

"Keep telling yourself that, Goldie. Maybe you'll start believing it. Although, I find that alcohol usually has the opposite effect on a woman's libido."

Hawk smirked and glanced at the beer in her hand, which she had been steadily emptying during their sparring without even realizing it. She'd nearly finished it, and it was starting to affect her head but not her wit.

"I see. So what you're saying is girls need to be drunk to find you attractive. That's totally understandable." Emily smirked right back.

Hawk shook his head. "You are cute when you try and fight with me. The question is why are you fighting this so hard, doll? I know you're attracted to me. You know you're attracted to me. You're leaving tomorrow. I'm leaving in about a week." He let the facts hang in the air for her to absorb and draw her own conclusions.

"Are you saying we should..." She could barely get the words out past the tightness his unspoken suggestion had caused in her throat.

"Have sex? Yup. I sure am." He grinned.

Could she do it? Did she want to? Have sex just for fun with a man she barely knew?

Although she did know him, didn't she? They'd spent two days together. She knew some of his personal and probably all of his military history from his file. She knew that for some reason, BB had chosen this man to represent the entire US Army. She could see that both Hawk's superiors and his subordinates liked him. All of that had to count for something.

"You sure are doing a lot of thinking in there, Goldie." Hawk ran one thick finger from her forehead, between her drawn brows and down her nose, tapping the tip playfully. "Stop frowning. You'll get wrinkles."

Emily fought the shiver that his touch sent down her spine and decided it wouldn't hurt to play along, for a bit anyway. "Let's say, under the influence of some sort of temporary insanity and German beer, that I did consider sleeping with you—"

"Oh, believe me, there'd be no sleeping. Just good old-fashioned sex. Incredible, unforgettable sex. Lots of it."

Emily swallowed hard. She didn't know if she'd ever experienced sex that qualified as that before. Certainly not in recent memory. She forced herself to focus on her point again.

"Anyway. If this were to happen, hypothetically of course, what would it mean?"

"What would it mean?" Hawk repeated.

"Yes, what would it mean?"

He laughed. "It would mean that you and I would both walk away satisfied. Me to Afghanistan, you to wherever you come from. It would mean that you would never have to deal with me and my brutish caveman ways again. However, you would have some damn nice memories to keep you warm at night. As would

I, and believe me, a year in Afghanistan with no sex, I'm going to need the memories."

"A year? Really?" Okay, so she'd gone a good year herself without sex, but Hawk didn't seem like the type to be celibate by choice.

"Doll, even if sex while deployed weren't against regulations, there aren't going to be any females where I'll be. Just those ten ugly mugs over there, and I don't go that way." Hawk glanced at his fellow soldiers and shook his head.

"So I could possibly be the last woman you were with? For a year?" Somehow knowing she could be the last woman he'd be with before going off to risk his life in the war got her all tingly. Patriotic even.

Sex for the good of the country. Supporting the troops took on a whole new meaning.

"Mmm hmm, and not just possibly. Most definitely. Tonight is our last hurrah. There won't be any time with getting ready to deploy to go out for beer or women. You're it, doll." He smiled and ran a hand up her arm. It sent a chill through her in spite of the hot, stale air in the bar. "The last woman I'll touch for an entire long, lonely year. The one I'll picture at night when I'm all alone in my cold, dark tent."

Emily drew a shaky breath. Her body wanted this man, and now her brain, which was usually the rational of the two, was starting to think it was a good idea too.

Hawk stepped closer. "Come on, doll. Do something just for the fun of it once in your life. Go tell your friend over there that you're tired and going back to your room."

She glanced at the group of soldiers surrounding Jai. "Even if I leave alone and you sneak upstairs later, they'll notice when you leave too. They'll all know."

"My men? Maybe. Probably. So what if they know? Do you really care? You'll never see any of them again, and they'll all be envying me spending one of our last nights in civilization with the prettiest girl in this place."

Damn, he was good. The caveman didn't talk often, but when he decided to, it was good stuff. She was really going to do this.

She took her last swallow of beer to bolster her nerves. "Room two ten at the hotel next door. Please try to be as discreet as you can so they don't know."

He looked about as surprised at her decision as she was herself. She'd shocked him. Emily took note of that with a smile, then turned to go lie to Jai. He'd most likely see right through her, but she had to make the attempt.

The worst part was what Hawk had said was true. At the moment, with her heart pounding and her sex throbbing, she couldn't really care what anyone thought about her tomorrow. She was only concerned with tonight.

Chapter Ten

Room two ten. Hawk swallowed hard and stared at the brass numbers on the door while the condoms purchased from the men's room at the Ratskeller felt heavy in his jeans pocket.

Once within the inner sanctum, Hawk's plan was to avoid talking at all costs. Emily was most likely the kind of woman to scare off easily. The last thing he wanted was for him to say something wrong and her to change her mind. He couldn't risk Emily turning tail and running. Not when he was this close. One thing Hawk knew for sure when it came to women, he never assumed he was in until he was, well, in.

Emily. Funny how now that he stood outside her hotel room, feet from her, moments from making last night's erotic dream come true, he didn't think of her as Goldilocks anymore. That was quite a change. Usually the women he slept with remained forever Red or Blondie or Legs or whatever name he'd dubbed them at first sight.

Maybe the difference was he and Emily had a professional relationship too. Who the hell knew? Nothing about this girl and his attraction to her made sense.

She wasn't his usual type. Hell, she was pretty much the exact opposite of it.

They fought like cats and dogs, and at times he was fairly sure she outright hated him. Yet here he was, outside her hotel room and at her invitation no less. Maybe the fighting was what made them so hot for each other.

Hawk realized he was wasting time on the wrong side of the door with all this thinking. Thinking. About a woman. That was also totally unlike him. He raised a fist and knocked loudly, holding his breath that she'd answer.

Answer she did. The door opened and Emily, still in the clothes she'd worn to the bar, stepped back to allow Hawk to enter. He took a step forward into the room and suddenly had an arm full of woman.

Good thing he had fast reflexes. He caught her and managed to not fall backward onto his ass as she dove at him. Wrapping her legs around his waist, she crashed her lips into his.

Hawk shouldered the door shut with the hope it would lock on its own. Angling his head to take full advantage of her hungry kiss, he didn't give the damn door another thought as Emily's tongue invaded his mouth.

Figuring they would end up there anyway, he stepped heavily toward the bed with Emily wrapped around his neck and waist. A willing woman literally in his hands was good, but one in the bed was even better. There he'd be free to unwrap the wool-covered package and enjoy what was underneath. More, holding her up was severely limiting his participation in this unexpectedly enthusiastic but more than welcome foreplay she'd initiated.

Hawk prided himself on the prowess of both his hands and mouth, and he intended to show off all his skills for this woman. They may have only one night together, but as he set her down and braced above her, he vowed he would make sure she never forgot it.

Beneath him on the mattress, Emily squirmed and broke their kiss. He raised himself up on shaky arms, afraid he had crushed her with his not-inconsiderable weight.

He needn't have worried.

All he could do was groan in response when one of her hands pulled at the turtleneck tucked into his jeans while the other fumbled with his fly.

"Clothes off."

She said only two breathless words. Two words were enough, and he couldn't agree more. He wanted them skin-to-skin. Since she was obviously willing, who was he to slow them down?

He'd get them both naked, but right now he craved her mouth again. With a long, low growl, he held her head and dove in for one more quick taste of her warm and inviting lips. Untangling his hand from the mass of her hair, he set to work on getting them undressed as fast as possible. She helped, and by the time his clothes were in a heap on the floor so were hers.

Then Hawk really had something to groan about. Her bulky sweater had hid more than just her soft, ivory skin. It also had disguised two perfectly shaped peaks tipped with rosy nipples.

"Damn, you're beautiful." To Hawk's surprise that was no bullshit. He meant every word.

"You're not so bad yourself," she whispered while her hands explored his now-bare chest.

From the top of her blonde head to the tips of her pale-pink polished toes, and everything in between, this woman was a man's wet dream. Better than Hawk's latest dream actually, because she was real, in more ways than one. All of her. Every last inch—right down to the patch of pale curls between her legs proving her a natural blonde—was God-given temptation.

He'd always been a boob man, usually the bigger the better. But after a run of chicks with plastic parts, everything from breast implants to surgically plumped lips, Emily's natural perfection was a huge turn-on.

Hawk ran his tongue over one tightly pebbled nipple and watched her shiver. He liked that reaction, a lot, so he took the bite-sized tidbit into his mouth and suckled hard. She groaned and lifted her spine off the bed to press farther into his mouth.

Damn. If the rest of her was equally as sensitive, they were both in for one hell of a wild ride. He could hardly wait. When Emily spread her legs to give him room to lie between them, he didn't hesitate. Heart pounding, Hawk nestled his throbbing erection against her folds.

Hard enough to drive nails with the thing, he nudged a bit and found her slick and ready. "You're so wet."

"I've been that way for two days now." Her voice came out sounding raspy.

They'd first met two days ago. She was finally admitting she'd wanted him from the very beginning. That knowledge was nearly his undoing.

Hawk held himself very still as he tried to resist plunging unprotected into her. The way he felt, he didn't trust himself to not lose it the minute he was inside this woman. The dead-last thing he needed was a little David Hawkins Junior running around back in the States while he was in Afghanistan chasing baddies through the mountains.

At the speed of light, Hawk grabbed the foil packet from the pocket of his jeans and covered himself.

He slid deep inside Emily with one sure stroke. Throwing her head back against the pillow, she groaned as he pushed inside. He'd never expected her to react so readily to his each and every touch. He was thrilled. And surprised. He should have known it was the ones you least expected it from who were the hottest in bed.

As he pulled out then slid back inside, Emily grabbed his hips and raised her own. Her eyes opened and he became caught in her blue gaze. It took him a second to realize he'd stopped all movement as he got lost in the depths of her heavily lidded eyes.

Shaking himself out of it, he reached down to raise her ass higher off the bed, then set a fast, hard pace. She was gasping in moments, her body clenching at his. He moved faster as her cries grew louder, until he felt her shatter around him. He couldn't help but watch her face as she came. So beautiful.

The woman always in control had lost control, and it was his doing. Both his ego and his cock swelled at the thought until a feeling touched his heart. Regret maybe. He wanted more of her than just this night.

Wanting what you couldn't have, especially on the eve of leaving for war, was a bad thing.

While she still gasped for breath and the aftershocks of her climax still gripped him, he pulled out. He flipped a boneless Emily over so she lay face down on the bed and he couldn't see that face that would surely haunt his dreams for the next year.

While her cries were muffled by the pillow, he plunged inside her. Hard and fast, over and over, he tried to lose himself in the act, rather than the woman. As her body met his thrust for thrust, he pounded himself to completion.

Hawk collapsed over Emily's heaving back. His head landed on the pillow next to hers and she angled her face toward his. The sounds of her breath filled his ear, the softness of her hair pillowed his cheek, her scent engulfed him and he knew he'd never forget any of it.

The man slept like the dead.

No sooner had he shuddered inside her, left to flush the condom and then slipped back between the covers he was out like a light. Not a word. Just silence, then unconsciousness. She'd felt him literally fall into sleep as the rock-like muscle-bound arm he'd thrown over her had gotten heavier and heavier, pinning her in place at his side.

Not that she blamed him for being physically worn out. He had expended quite a bit of energy. It wasn't like he'd left her unsatisfied and wanting or anything. No, she'd done quite a bit of shuddering herself. But still, how could he fall asleep so fast and so soundly?

His even breathing told her he certainly wasn't spending any time on second thoughts about what had happened between them. Emily glanced at the clock. She'd been second guessing herself and what had happened for an hour and a half now.

On top of not being able to sleep, she had to pee. Back in New York, counting the days until she met her supposed Prince Charming, Emily had imagined a similar scenario. Snuggling in bed after making love, bodies intertwined, falling asleep in his arms feeling warm, safe and loved. Nowhere in her visions had it been a one-night stand, and in her dreams she hadn't had to desperately relieve herself.

Waiting any longer was not an option. It would just be too bad if she woke Sleeping Beauty. Emily wiggled her way free of the vise that was Hawk's arm and slipped from the bed.

When she returned from the bathroom, she found he hadn't moved a muscle. Some war-hardened, trained fighter he was. She could probably set off a bomb under the bed and he wouldn't wake up.

"Sure hope the Taliban doesn't sneak up on you at night or you're a goner," she whispered and crawled back under the warm covers with a shiver.

"I heard that."

She could hear the smile in his voice.

"Well, it's true. You sleep like a rock."

"Yes. When I know it's safe to do so. Otherwise the slightest sound—a boot crunching, a breath taken too deeply—will wake me up. Believe me."

Hawk readjusted his position to accommodate her reentry to the bed. With her back against his front, he flung his arm over her waist.

"Oh."

What else could she say about that? She knew nothing about what this man went through on a daily basis and she probably never would. Another reason her decision to jump him, literally, and hop right into bed was probably ill advised. Mistake or not, as long as she'd done it once, she might as well do it again. If he was up for it.

Emily wiggled back against him. "Speaking of sleeping, what was all that talk in the bar about how there'd be no sleeping tonight? Hmm?"

"I have an excuse. You wore me out. I didn't know Goldilocks would turn into the Big Bad Wolf in bed." Two big arms gathered her up and pulled her closer to his chest. As he started to kiss up and down her neck and shoulder she felt him grow hard against her naked butt.

"You're mixing your fairytales." Emily sighed as the physical sensations sweeping through her from his touch battled with her emotions.

She'd been more forward with Hawk than she'd ever been with any other man in her past, as few of them as there'd been. What he must think of her after that. She hated to even think about it.

"What's bothering you, doll? I can feel you frowning from here."

"I'm wondering how stupid sleeping with you was. I don't usually do this, you know." It wasn't exactly easy to think with his naked body pressed against her, making her warm inside and out, but she managed to answer the question.

"Do what? Have incredible sex with irresistible soldiers you've only known for two days?"

"Yes. The two-day part, at least. The irresistible part is pushing it, don't you think?" Sparring with Hawk brought Emily back into her comfort zone.

He chuckled against her back. "You still don't like the idea that you wanted me from the minute you walked into that office, do you?"

Actually, it was from the minute his eyes had stared back at her from the computer printout back in New York, but she wasn't telling him that. And because of that instant attraction, she should have run from the Ratskeller the moment she realized Hawk was inside.

She'd fallen half in love with Hawk before ever meeting him, imagining a fairytale happy ever after with her Army prince. Even the reality of two days of fighting with him over every detail of this campaign hadn't squelched that attraction. So what had she gone and done? She jumped into bed with him, willing to settle for one night over nothing at all.

Stupid, stupid, stupid.

"You're doing it again." His voice was low and deep.

"Doing what?"

"Thinking."

He was right. She was thinking, because having sex with Hawk brought up a good dozen or so questions. Would she ever hear from him again? If she did have to contact him again for work, how weird would it be? What if he got injured or killed? Worse, what if he was just fine but she still never heard from him again?

"I can't help it." Emily sighed.

"Well, I can." He skimmed his hand from her waist to her hip, and then down to her thigh. There, he paused and made small circles against her skin.

"You can what? Not think? Yeah, I figured that."

"No, my witty little thinker. I meant I can stop you from thinking."

His large, rough hand pulled her leg up and over his hip. With her spread wide, he found her clit and began stroking. Her eyes closed involuntarily as he worked her increasingly sensitive spot. The tension began to build and she breathlessly shuddered out a moan.

"Still thinking?" He nipped at her neck after delivering that question against her ear.

"Shut up, Hawk." With her body coiling, tensing for release, her rapid breathing should have given him his answer.

Hawk chuckled just as the hip-bucking orgasm broke over her.

She was still quivering when he covered himself and slid inside her. Then Hawk wasn't laughing any longer. There was no joking, no more talking at all, as he set a fast pace. After a few incredibly wonderful minutes of him thrusting into her, his grip tightened on her hips. With a deep groan that reverberated straight through her body, he came. She felt him throb inside her.

He laid his head against hers, breathing heavily behind her. "Damn. I could happily do that again right now, but we both need a shower first. I've got some tasty plans for more fun and I want us both extra clean for it."

Emily groaned in protest, not at the idea of more sex, but that it meant getting out of the warm bed again. Germans needed to turn up the thermostats in their hotels. Keeping a room this cold was barbaric. "Now? It's cold out there."

"Yes, now. And don't you worry about being cold. I'll warm you up. Believe me." He grabbed her hand and pulled her up and out of the blessed warmth of the sheets.

Emily glanced down and took in his spectacularly naked, beautifully muscular form. The thick thighs, small waist and indescribably large forearms. She imagined him bracing her against the wall of the shower stall as he plunged inside her. Oh boy.

Just the mere thought of sex with Hawk again had her heart racing, and they'd just finished. It couldn't be good to want a man this much, especially when she'd probably never see him again.

"Are you sure you don't want to go back to sleep? You seemed pretty tired before." Nerves had Emily resorting to teasing him.

Well on the way to being hard again, Hawk took a step closer until their bodies touched. "I think we're done sleeping for the night. What about you?"

Not having even closed her eyes yet, forget about getting any sleep, Emily still nodded in agreement.

She had only one night with this man. She would make the most of it and deal with the consequences later.

Chapter Eleven

Afghanistan—the most heavily mined place in the world—and for better or worse, Hawk's home for the next year. He got his first glimpse of the desolate region in the dim light of dusk.

The plane carrying him, his squad and their loaded pallet of gear landed without incident at the old Kandahar International Airport, now being used as the base airfield. Having secured a seat in the front row of the C14 aircraft, Hawk's boots hit the ground ahead of his men as he took his first step onto Afghan soil. The blast of frigid air in his face served as the local welcoming committee.

Kandahar was only the initial stop on their tour of Afghanistan. Next up, Bagram Air Base, then a quick hop on a helicopter to their final destination, the mountainous outskirts of Kabul, where the insurgents waited for them. He had no doubt the baddies would be very sorry to see them arrive.

Hawk and his men had gotten their official Afghan primer back at Hohenfels, but during their quick welcome tour of the base at Kandahar, he realized that actually being here, seeing the sights, listening to the stories and first-hand experiences of the Army guys who'd already been here, was quite an eye opener.

The base at Kandahar was riddled with crashed Russian helicopters from the war in the eighties. Even the rafters for the roof of one of the buildings was made from old Russian helicopter blades. The base was at a high altitude and there were mountains off in the distance everywhere he looked.

Hawk discovered there were some very cool things about Kandahar—an opinion he was beginning to reevaluate as he sat in the dining hall during chow and got an earful from one of the guys stationed here.

"When they talk about landmines, they ain't shitting you. There are old landmines everywhere outside the fence." The soldier from the 10th Mountain Division dropped that information before casually scooping up some potatoes.

Landmines. That was enough to make Hawk lose his appetite for the boiled carrots, mashed potatoes and ketchup-covered meatloaf littering his plate. But since he had no intention of venturing outside the fence during his brief stopover, it shouldn't be an issue—for here and for today at least. Who knew what surprises the region he was heading to held?

"So there are a bunch of Canadian troops here, huh?" Wally talked right through a mouthful of macerated meat.

Across the table, their welcoming party of one nodded. "Yup. But there are a lot of US Army units too. The main ground force is from the 10th Mountain like me. The Army aviation units attached to us are from all over. There's a lot of reserve units on base as well."

"I was told to expect a lot of snow where we're heading." Unlike Wally, Pettit asked his question before he shoved another forkful of food into his mouth.

The soldier let out a snort. "Snow? Yeah, there's snow, and cold, but that's nothing compared to what it's like here in the summer."

Wally took one glance at the expression of concern on Pettit's face and laughed. "I'm from Alabama. I can handle the heat."

The soldier shook his head. "The heat's not the issue. Don't get me wrong, it's hot, but the humidity's not like in the south. It's more of a dry heat. The problem's the sand. It's baby-powder fine and boy, does it blow. There are sandstorms all the time in summer. Damn stuff gets into everything. Feels like I'm always cleaning it out of my damn weapon."

Four-foot snowstorms that hit overnight in winter and sandstorms every day in summer. Lovely. Hawk never thought he'd find a place that made Iraq look appealing, but he may have done just that. Thank you, Uncle Sam for the all-expenses-paid year-long vacation in Hell.

"Don't worry too much about the weather though. It's the locals you really need to watch out for. We pay off the warlords to allow our convoys to drive back and forth to our forward operating base."

As the soldier kept talking, what he said had Hawk laying down his fork and knife so he could give the unbelievable tale his full attention.

Wally's eyes opened wide. "I've heard rumors about the locals doing some sick shit, like hiding IEDs in corpses so when the soldiers go to investigate the body they get blown to kingdom come."

"That's no rumor. It's fact. These guys are crazy bastards. A few years back a local warlord who was on our side, probably because we paid him enough to be, skinned a local alive for attacking American soldiers and hung his body on a post for everyone to see as an example."

Hawk shook his head in horrified disbelief. "Shit."

"Jesus." Pettit hissed under his breath.

"I know. It's the stuff of movies, but it's real. Hey, you can see the house and compound belonging to one of the warlords from the fences at the airfield. Ask someone to point it out to you when you leave."

All just part of the Kandahar sightseeing tour Hawk supposed. He let out a sigh as he wondered exactly what the chances were he and all his guys would get out of Afghanistan alive. A year from now, how many would be coming back through Kandahar on the journey home with all their parts in working order?

He'd thought more than a few times about what he'd like to do with sweet little Emily when he finally got home next year, and then he'd thought better of it. Now, hearing the horror stories, he was even more certain. His decision to avoid anything more was the correct choice.

Hawk didn't need the image of Emily crying for him back home distracting him downrange. She was probably pissed as hell at him. He'd only emailed her that once, and even then he'd kept it short. But that was for the best.

In the end, she would thank him...if he was around to be thanked. Having a relationship while deployed was too hard for both parties involved. Hawk needed one hundred and ten percent of his attention on the job. Not on her.

If she was still available, and if he was still alive, he'd deal with her anger when he got back Stateside. The vision of tempering an angry Emily put a smile on his face. Hawk tucked that little scenario away to enjoy later when he was in the semi-privacy of their temporary lodging for the night. But right now, he needed to arm himself with as much info as he could to make sure he got both himself and his men home.

Hawk turned his attention back to the soldier across from him. "What else have you heard about what's waiting for us in those mountains in the Kabul Province? Whatever you can tell me, I wanna hear. All of it."

Emily walked into the meeting late, which was not her fault at all.

Someone had fallen onto the subway tracks, so they'd stopped service to rescue the stupid person. She felt justified in calling the person an idiot because they weren't hurt and really, who leans so far over the tracks to see if the train is coming that they actually fall in unless they are brain dead?

Anyway, her train had been late. Consequently, so was she for a meeting with Katie and the big bosses—the owners of the agency—aka the guys who signed her paycheck. These guys were important.

She was sticking with blaming the subway. It didn't matter that she lived near enough to walk if she absolutely had to for any reason, like the trains not running. But it was a long walk and cold outside, and she had on her new red patent-leather shoes and there were a ton of puddles from a recent rainstorm.

Emily tried not to think about how she had been running late that morning anyway after having slept like crap the night before because she was once again reliving her one night with Hawk.

Her brain knew thinking about him was pointless. It should anyway, she told it enough. Yet the rebellious gray matter continued to disobey the minute the lights went out at night. She had no control over it.

Apparently, Emily looked as flustered as she felt as she burst in and interrupted the conversation in progress.

"Sorry." Cringing, she flung her bulging briefcase on the conference table while at the same time offering that hurried apology.

Mr. Howard, as in the Howard & Dean Agency, nodded in her direction but didn't say anything about it. Hopefully that was a good thing, Emily wasn't sure.

Katie smiled sympathetically and said loud enough for everyone to hear, "Tough ride in?"

Thank goodness for Katie, smoothing things over. Emily answered with a short laugh. "They actually stopped the subway for like an hour for somebody on the tracks, but I'm here now. Ready to get to it."

"You're just in time." Mr. Dean, the other half of the partnership, resumed the meeting. "We were about to review preliminary results of the Army campaign. The client reports they've tracked a small spike in recruitment since the new Army ads hit. However—"

Uh, oh. Howevers were never good.

"—it's not nearly as large a response as the SpecOps ads yielded last year. We need to evaluate why that is. Any ideas, people?" Mr. Dean glanced at the employees assembled expectantly.

Katie shrugged. "I'd have to say that I'm not sure we can expect the same level of response. It's apples and oranges trying to compare SpecOps and enlisted Army. We portrayed SpecOps as elite, which made people want it more."

Mr. Howard nodded. "That's exactly why we didn't take the same approach to the Army campaign. Our goal, which was successful in some respects and not so in others, is to show the Army soldier as a warrior, a protector of our freedom, yet at the same time, make it so that young men and woman can identify with him. Relate to him. See themselves in his shoes...or rather combat boots. Todd, the ad please."

Mr. Howard's assistant, Todd, instantly held up one of the print ads. Suddenly Hawk's piercing eyes bore directly into Emily as she stared at the glossy photograph before her.

Her traitorous heart began beating faster.

The perfect tag-team player, Mr. Dean took over where his partner had left off. "Take a look at this ad. Our man has the terrifying-warrior look down pat. The question is how do we make him appear more accessible to the average man and woman?"

Katie sat up straighter in her chair and pushed aside the ever-present box of crackers she ate to combat the morning sickness. She kept it next to her at all times now since she'd decided to reveal her pregnancy to the entire company.

"Perhaps that's the difference in the response. Accessibility. BB did a press tour as the SpecOps ads hit. National television appearances on the morning talk shows, local radio stations in targeted areas, live appearances. We're also missing the advantage of being connected to a big name. Remember, we piggy-backed the recruitment ads on top of a national Andre Milano underwear campaign starring BB."

Howard and Dean nodded as one.

Emily nearly choked.

Hawk was unhappy about posing for her in his uniform. She shuddered to think how he would react if they decided he had to pose in designer underwear. She cringed at the thought of having to tell Hawk he was going to be interviewed by the five chattering ladies of *The View*, like BB had so willingly been.

She had to put a stop to this, and now.

Emily raised her hand tentatively to speak. She was used to being the assistant, sitting silently, taking notes, supplying what Katie needed just like Mr. Howard's assistant, Todd, and Mr. Dean's assistant, Marci. She was not used to being an active participant, but as this was her assignment, she had to speak up.

Mr. Dean noted her raised hand and bobbed his head in her direction with an amused smile. "Emily?"

"Hawk, um, Staff Sergeant Hawkins, the model, is currently deployed in Afghanistan. We would have to get the approval of his superior officers to have him sent home for that kind of press tour." Nervous, Emily spoke quickly, hoping all the while that the words *I had sex with the model* weren't emblazoned in red across her forehead.

"I don't think there's a need to have him sent back here." Mr. Howard shook his head slowly. "Afghanistan is perfect. Do the tour over there."

Emily could almost see the wheels of his mind turning as the idea formed.

She frowned. "But there's a war on. I'm not sure I can get a United States soldier booked on *Good Day, Afghanistan,* even if they are on our side."

Her little joke earned her a frown from Mr. Howard. "I don't expect you to. We need to show this soldier in his element, not sitting around drinking coffee and chatting with some show's hostess. I want him eating with his men, working out at the base, training. Or, you know, a video of him handing out dolls or chocolate or whatever to the little Afghan kiddies."

Mr. Dean nodded vigorously. "That would cover the other aspect of this campaign. The client wants the market to realize the Army's focus is the people over there. Giving the war a face the public can relate to is just as important as giving the Army a relatable personality. I think it's a great idea."

Hawk wasn't exactly a relatable personality.

"I do have to agree with Emily on one point. There is a war on." Katie jumped into the conversation. "Hawkins is a professional soldier and is already over there. But we'd have to send over Emily and at least one cameraman, ideally two, one for still shots and one for video. As untrained civilians, can we keep all of them safe? I've heard conditions can get pretty bad in some spots."

Emily's hopes rose. If anyone could get them out of this mess, it was Katie. Though when she considered the dangers in Afghanistan, she had to think that living in New York City was probably pretty good training.

"The USO sends people to the war zone all the time. Important people too. Celebrities. Robin Williams just got back and that Irish Tenor guy. There are always bands and singers over there performing for the troops at their bases." Todd suddenly joined the conversation. He was obviously feeling bold since Emily, also an assistant, had spoken up earlier.

Emily frowned at him, willing him to shut up.

The last thing she had expected was to ever see Hawk again. The bastard hadn't even bothered to email her lately and say he was still alive. Given that, she was not in any rush to fly to Afghanistan and have to work with him. He obviously didn't want to see or talk to her or he would have emailed. And besides further bruising her wounded ego, flying into the middle of the war hadn't been on her immediate agenda either.

"Perfect. Great idea, Todd." Mr. Howard smiled at his underling, who glowed under the praise, probably while he envisioned getting his own big solo assignment and moving up in the company.

"Marci." Mr. Dean turned to his assistant who sat silently with her laptop open on the conference table clicking away as she took notes for him. "What can you find about the USO?"

Marci's fingers flew into action and didn't it figure, she had the website up in no time.

"They are a not-for-profit, privately-owned organization. Ooo, this is good. They offer what they call a 'handshake tour'. Besides comedians and musical acts, they've had authors, sports figures and politicians on tour. Here's a picture of that bicyclist Lance Armstrong with the troops. It says they have a USO center set up at Bagram Air Base in Afghanistan."

"Where is our boy Hawk?" Mr. Dean asked Emily directly, shocking her out of her trance.

"Kabul," she reluctantly supplied, feeling her cheeks blush at the mention of *our* boy Hawk.

"Marci. How close is that to Bagram?" Mr. Dean asked.

"I think they're pretty close." Know-it-all Todd jumped in once again uninvited.

Emily sat silently as Marci's fingers clicked, knowing damn well after already obsessively studying the Afghan map that Bagram and Kabul were very close, on the map at least.

Before Marci could tell them that, Emily's hand shot up again. "But Hawk isn't a celebrity like Lance Armstrong. Why would the soldiers want to shake hands with just another soldier?"

Mr. Howard answered her. "We're not trying to make Hawk a celebrity among other soldiers, but we do want them to relate to him and feel good that he's representing them to the world. But more importantly, this tour is a photo op. It's for the people back home who need to feel good about where their young men and women and hard-earned tax dollars are going. Photos and videos of him there, properly placed in the media here at home, will accomplish that."

"Bagram Air Base is an hour drive north of the capital city of Kabul, Mr. Dean." Marci looked absolutely gleeful at finding that out for her boss.

Damn efficient Marci.

This could not happen. They had agreed in the bar before any of the incredible sex they would never see each other again. He hadn't made contact since landing in Afghanistan so she had to assume he hadn't changed his mind.

Emily simply could not face seeing Hawk and having him blow her off, not after he'd occupied her mind night and day for weeks now. Besides that, he didn't even want his men to know about the print ads, and now her bosses wanted him to conduct a celebrity handshake tour. He'd flip out over that and probably take it out on her. She had to stop this runaway train.

"Hawk isn't in the city. I believe he and his soldiers are in a primitive camp somewhere in the Kabul Province in the mountains along the Pakistan border." Emily realized too late that was an awful lot of information for her to have about a model she'd worked with only once.

Mr. Howard raised an eyebrow, his coffee mug poised halfway to his lips. "I take it you can get in touch with him somehow?"

Emily blanched. She'd emailed him once while he was still in Germany. After his response, she'd had no intention of ever doing it again.

"Um, I don't know. I suppose so. I can try emailing him, but the satellite internet can be iffy there...I believe." Yeah, she didn't sound too much like she'd become a stalker and read everything she could get her hands on regarding the troops in that area. "But again, it will be up to his superiors to allow him to come to Bagram."

"The client is the US Army." Mr. Dean tapped his copy of the client folder on the conference table. "If they want their own campaign to succeed, I don't see that they'd have a problem working with us by loaning out one soldier for a few days."

"True," Mr. Howard agreed. "But it never hurts to cover all the bases when dealing with the military." He swiveled his chair to face Katie. "How about your contacts? Can you get this Hawk ordered to do a USO handshake tour?"

Katie smiled. "I'll call Hank Miller from CentCom and see what he can do. That man is amazing when it comes to getting people to do things."

Mr. Howard donned a satisfied smile. He loved nothing more than pulling strings. "Excellent."

Smiling too, Mr. Dean nodded. "This may actually work out perfectly. If we can hook him up with a celebrity already on a scheduled tour, we can piggyback on their publicity and the troop support. There's our missing star power that we had with the Milano-SpecOps joint campaign. Marci, can you forward the USO information to Emily?"

"Already emailed. And they have contact information and phone numbers listed right here on the site."

Oh goody. "Thanks, Marci." Emily tried to sound sincere.

Mr. Dean started shuffling papers into a pile and stashing them into various folders, which he shoved at Todd. "Emily? Can you handle coordinating the USO aspect?"

"Yes, sir. I'll get right on it."

"Great. Keep us informed." Mr. Dean clicking the latch on his briefcase closed sounded to Emily like the final nail in her coffin.

"This is an important client," Mr. Howard added, as if Emily didn't already know that paralyzing detail. "I want to be apprised every step of the way."

With that, Howard and Dean both rose and the meeting was over.

As the room emptied, Emily remained frozen in her seat. This was going to happen. She would have to see him again, do her job and do it well and all while pretending that everything was perfectly okay.

For maybe the thousandth time since Germany, Emily revisited her and Hawk's final moments together.

"You going to be able to get back to the base okay?" she'd asked that morning, suitcase packed and zipped and ready to go to the airport.

"Yeah, I kept one of the cars we came in and made the rest of the guys cram into the other two." Hawk had run a hand up her arm to cup her face and then said, "You know, I've been thinking."

"Uh, oh. Are you sure that's safe? You thinking?" Emily had teased him to avoid tearing up at their parting.

He'd grinned at her then, and she remembered her heart skipping a beat. That was when she'd known saying goodbye and meaning it was not going to be as easy.

"I was thinking that it might be kind of cool if you did email me the pictures. I'd like to have them, you know, just for fun. Might be good for a laugh." Hawk's words had made her heart and her hopes surge.

She'd nodded. "Oh, sure. I can definitely do that. No problem."

Yeah sure, no problem at all, except that she'd emailed him the pictures the moment her feet hit US soil and had gotten exactly one word back from him by email. "Thanks." That was it.

And that is what she got for hoping, for planning, for thinking that an agreed-upon one-night stand could be anything more.

"You gonna be okay with this? Em?"

Emily was yanked away from her memories with a jolt. Katie had been talking to her. "Hmm?"

"Going to Afghanistan, into a war zone? Are you okay with that?" Katie clarified when Emily gave her a blank stare.

"Oh yeah. I'm great. Actually, I've always wanted to see Afghanistan." Emily joked to cover her discomposure.

"You sure?" Concern was clear on Katie's face.

"Yeah. I'm sure." Compared to seeing Hawk again, the war was the least of Emily's worries.

"Are you going to email Hawk with the good news?"

The question was perfectly innocent. Katie knew nothing about Emily's night with Hawk. Katie had no clue how much she dreaded having to contact Hawk since she'd chosen to keep her little indiscretion in Germany to herself.

"Um, I think I'll get everything ironed out first with the USO and wait to get approval from the Army. No use getting Hawk involved if we might have to cancel." With any luck they wouldn't get approval. Emily felt like a traitor to her company for wishing that, but it was true.

Katie nodded. "You're right. I'll be interested to see how the USO feels about our idea."

The other question remaining was exactly how angry Hawk was going to be about this. It wasn't going to be good.

Chapter Twelve

"Can I borrow your toothpaste later, Hawk?" Wally asked after a mouthful of food. "I'm out until my next care package gets here from Mama."

Whenever the hell the next supply drop would be.

Hawk sighed. "Yeah, sure."

Wally grinned. "Thanks. I've got an extra deodorant if you need it."

Hawk raised a brow. "Thanks."

If the temperature reached above freezing in the near future, Wally's antiperspirant might be a hot commodity, but at the moment the chance of sweating seemed pretty slim.

Personal items at their forward operating base in the Kabul Province were scarce, to put it mildly.

Hawk and his squad were far from anyone else, including their own unit. No base meant no store, which meant some basic necessities, things like toothpaste and, believe it or not, forks, were hard to come by. Guys actually walked around with their forks in their pockets to make sure they didn't lose them or no one swiped them.

You pretty much had to come stocked with everything you would need, borrow from one of the other guys or do without until more arrived from home. Hawk's camp was so remote that supplies were sling loaded beneath a chopper, flown in and then dropped. Unfortunately, you never knew when the supply drop would arrive. Or exactly where it would end up crashing to the ground.

It seemed the only convenience they did have on a regular basis was internet access. Go figure. A hell of a lot of good email did Hawk since he'd vowed to himself he wouldn't maintain contact with Emily while he was downrange.

Basically, it seemed the only things to do there were fight, write—for those who had someone to write to—clean weapons or reload mags. Fun stuff.

Oh, and think.

There was far too much time to think. More often than not, Hawk's thoughts turned to Emily and their one night together. Then his mind went to that day right after they'd been together when she'd emailed him in Germany with his photos.

She'd kept the email all casual and light, on the surface anyway. Reading between the lines, Hawk could tell she wanted more. He could have a girlfriend if he wanted one. He knew he could have Emily if he wanted her.

Wanting wasn't the problem.

This was not the time or place to get himself tied to a new girl back in the States. Every moment of every day had to be spent making sure he brought his men home alive. After he'd accomplished that, God willing, he'd worry about the other parts of his life. Hawk yanked his mind away from thoughts of Emily.

He stood and sent a meaningful look at Wally. "I'm gonna go get on the computer and email my sister for some toothpaste. Looks like I'll be needing some more soon."

"Ask her to send some pictures of herself too." Wally grinned and waggled his eyebrows.

The man knew exactly how to push Hawk's buttons. Hawk ignored him. Hopefully, like an ill-behaved child, Wally would give up if he didn't get a reaction.

With a sigh, Hawk threw away his empty MRE package— meals ready to eat being their main sustenance nowadays—and left his men to finish their respective meals.

He made his way to the tent where the shared computer was located. Since the rest of the guys were still eating, he was alone as he logged into his email account. He owed his sister an email anyway or there would be hell to pay. It was just easier to shoot her a quick hello than listen to her bitch for the rest of his life.

As expected, an email from her sat in his inbox. *Would be nice to know my brother is alive and well. Write me! Susan*

Also, as per usual, were a good dozen jokes, pictures or funny videos sent to him by the guys back at the rear. Hawk deleted most of those without reading them.

Buried below all the others, one message had his hand pausing on the mouse as his pulse sped.

After all this time, there was an email from Emily. Hawk clicked it open. He found himself leaning closer to the screen to read it.

Hawk. You'll be getting orders for another assignment. I swear I did my best to get you out of it. Sorry. Emily.

What the hell? Orders for another modeling assignment? Out here?

Hawk laughed. If they could get those orders to him through the snowdrifts, he'd gladly follow them. Emily probably wanted a picture of him in his white snow camo *outfit*. She'd have him standing outside in a blizzard for some new ad, as if that would make the young boys and girls back home jump right up and run to the local recruiting office to join up.

Since it was doubtful they were sending Rasta-photographer here to him, Hawk figured whatever pictures she needed he could have Pettit take.

Hawk would have Pettit snap a few shots with that super expensive digital camera the man was so proud of. Then he'd email the pictures to Emily and be done with it. That should cover it.

Confident that was all this new assignment would entail, Hawk sent a quick reply to his sister, remembering to ask her to send him toothpaste, and a package of plastic forks if she had the time to pick them up. Then he emptied all the remaining emails out of his inbox and logged off.

Back in his tent, Hawk broke down his weapon and took out the gun oil and supplies he'd need. He settled in for the meticulous task of cleaning the familiar item.

The act was almost like meditation for him. As his hands completed the task they knew so well, he let his mind wander. As usual, Emily was the main attraction.

Chuckling, Hawk imagined Emily's horror at having to ask him for more pictures when she knew how unhappy he'd been about the first set.

Then he heard it, far in the distance. The familiar *whoop whoop whoop* of blades cutting air had him on immediate alert. Hawk's gaze snapped to locate his backup weapon as he slammed the pieces of the gun in his hand back together, until he heard the jubilant shouts of his guys. He relaxed. It definitely wasn't an attack.

"Woo hoo! Mail call." Outside, someone, it sounded like Wally, shouted the announcement.

Slamming the last piece of his cleaned and oiled weapon into place, Hawk flung it over his shoulder and went out to see what goodies had been delivered. Hopefully Wally's care package with his toothpaste and maybe even Hawk's mysterious new orders would be among the packages and letters.

He chuckled again and thought of Emily trying to get him out of the new assignment. Perhaps she wasn't too angry with him and his lack of communications after all.

In her peripheral vision, Emily noticed Jai glancing at her once again, just like he'd been doing for most of the flight. "What?"

Jai shrugged. "Nothing. You just seem nervous."

"I'm not nervous." That said, Emily noticed she'd been drumming her fingers on the armrest between their two seats and immediately folded both hands in her lap over her seat belt.

"It's perfectly understandable, Em. You're flying to Afghanistan. The war may have begun centered in Iraq, but there's a major threat in Afghanistan. It's no picnic. I remember my first time here. It can be scary, and even more so for you being a woman."

She rolled her eyes. "We're going to be on a US base full of armed men. I'm not worried I'll be taken hostage by the local gun-toting bad guys. Honestly."

It was only one guy who had her on edge.

"Hmm." Jai's doubt was clearly evident in that one sound.

"Yes? Do you have more to say?" She turned in her narrow commercial-airplane seat to face Jai.

Even in business class, the seats were not exactly comfortable for the length of time they'd been in them. But right now, Jai was even more annoying than Emily's seat and the stiffness in her butt and legs.

"I was just remembering the flight home from Germany. You were a little freaky then too, exhausted and hyper at the same time."

Memories of why that was true hit her hard. She threw up her defenses to distract Jai. "I'm not afraid of flying if that's what you're saying."

"No, I know it's not fear of flying. I've flown with you before and you were fine. But there's something..." Realization dawned on his face. "It's him. You're nervous about seeing him again."

She felt her face blanch. "I don't know who you're talking about."

Emily looked anywhere except at Jai. She was such a bad liar that people always saw right through her, and she didn't need Jai knowing the truth. Not now on the way to see Hawk again when she was already beyond stressed.

"Oh my God. You had sex with Hawk that last night in Germany. The night we went to the bar and he was there."

Emily nearly choked. Was it written that clearly across her face? "What? No, of course not."

"I can't believe I didn't realize it before." Jai continued on, studying her face as she felt it grow hot.

"Jai, I don't know what you're talking about."

"Em, come on." He let out a long, slow hiss of breath. "The sexual tension between you and Hawk during those photo shoots and then at the bar was so thick I could have cut it with a knife. I just never imagined you'd actually... Wow. You and Hawk."

Heart pounding, Emily started to deny it some more but instead sank low in her seat, defeated. "You must think so badly of me."

Frowning, Jai let out a short laugh. "Why?"

"I barely knew him."

"Oh jeez, Em. Do you know what I see on the road with all those models and crew? One-night stands are the tamest thing compared to the orgies, drugs, alcohol—you name it and I've seen it. You finally letting yourself relax for a night and falling for a really nice guy is nothing to be ashamed of."

"You think Hawk is nice?" That out of all the rest surprised her the most.

"Yeah. I mean, in a tough-guy trained-killer kind of way."

"You really think so?"

"Yeah, I do. He's a good guy."

"How do you know?"

"Don't forget, I spent time with his squad at the Ratskeller after both you and Hawk mysteriously got tired about the same time and went to bed." Jai obviously realized now that excuse had been a big old fib.

She rubbed her hands over her face. "I told him to wait awhile so it wouldn't look suspicious."

"Oh, he did. Hawk waited a good three minutes." Jai grinned. "Anyway, I can tell you his men love him. You want some guy advice, Em?"

Emily guessed it couldn't hurt. "Sure."

"If you want to know if a man is worth your time, you look at how he treats others and how they treat him, particularly his subordinates. Hawk's a decent man. A bit serious at times, but still, you could have done far worse than him to jump in bed with."

Emily sighed. As much as she would love to tell Jai how wrong he was about Hawk, she couldn't bring herself to admit he hadn't even bothered to email her after she wrote him about this assignment.

Hawk may well be a good guy to his soldiers. She'd freely admit that, but so what if he was a man's man? In the female department, and at communicating, the man was severely lacking. In fact, he just plain sucked. Nice guys returned emails. Case closed.

"Can we change the subject now?"

He smirked but nodded. "Sure. Hmm. Let's see. Subject change. Oh, I know. So what do you think of Little Miss USO up there?" Jai suggested the new topic of conversation in a low whisper.

"I think, judging from the looks of her outfit, the soldiers at Bagram are going to be very happy to see her." Emily wasn't so considerate and used her natural voice level, figuring Little Miss USO and her entourage probably couldn't hear. Not from their seats all the way up there in first class where she was probably drinking bottles of complimentary champagne.

Honestly, a tube top for a plane ride to Afghanistan?

"She's an entertainer, Emily. They all act a bit over the top. It's just part of the image. You know, packaging for the public."

Emily raised a brow, thinking that the *packaging* had a little help from a bottle of red hair dye and some silicone implants, not to mention a press person, makeup person and bruiser of a bodyguard.

"So you're saying the fact she flirted with you is all part of the act?"

Jai grinned. "Nope, that was all part of my charm."

"And what about her flirting with the pilot, the man who took our boarding passes and even the gay male flight attendant? Hmm?" Emily challenged.

"She did? I'm crushed." Jai feigned shock, and then laughed at Emily's scowl. "All right, I'll admit it. She is a bit flirty."

And Hawk was scheduled to be at her side every step of his time in Bagram. Just great. Emily imagined all the flirting, or worse, Little Miss USO would do with Hawk and how he'd eat it right up.

She let out a low groan.

"Oh, lighten up, Em. This being part of a USO tour will be fun. You'll see."

Emily laughed bitterly. "Oh yeah, real fun. I can't wait."

Chapter Thirteen

Emily's love for Kerri London, chart-topping country singer and star of this USO thing, did not grow during the twenty-two-hour journey from New York. In fact, by the time their plane landed in Afghanistan and Emily waited in the aisle for what seemed like forever for Little Miss USO's entourage to get all of her many carry-ons out of the overhead compartments, she was seething with anger.

"Some people are so inconsiderate. Why the hell didn't she check all that stuff with the regular luggage instead of carrying it on?" Emily complained to Jai.

He glanced down at Emily's laptop case and additional briefcase and raised an eyebrow.

"I needed this stuff to work on the flight," she defended against his unspoken condemnation. So she'd been so nervous about seeing Hawk again she hadn't done a damn thing, but still, she'd intended to and that's all that counted.

Jai laughed. "Okay, if you say so. Come on. It looks like we're moving. I've had quite enough of riding around in this tin can."

"Hmm. A bit of claustrophobia?" Emily jumped on the opportunity to pay Jai back for his teasing of her.

He shot her a look. "I admit nothing. And before you start picking on me, let's see how you fare on your first helicopter ride, shall we?"

Jai headed down the aisle. Emily followed a bit less enthusiastically. She'd thought the incredibly long and many-legged trip to the airport in Kabul had been bad, but she had a feeling the relatively short helicopter ride to the military airport at Bagram Air Base would probably be far worse.

She was right in that prediction. White knuckled the entire time, Emily managed to not lose her lunch or pass out during her first helicopter ride, but she was shaking like a leaf by the time they got off. Jai on the other hand, didn't seem to mind it at all.

"So you don't like being on a huge commercial jet, but you didn't mind this flying eggbeater? Why is that?" She frowned as she stumbled after him on wobbly legs across the airfield.

Jai shrugged. "We all have our little quirks. And that huge commercial jet, as you put it, doesn't feel so huge when you're as tall as I am. My legs are still cramped. Next trip, we're going to have to get the big guys to spring for first class."

She let out a laugh. "Yeah, good luck. Maybe for talent but not for us."

Speaking of first class, Emily glanced back at Little Miss USO. She was doing just fine as both her bodyguard and some military guy helped her out of the helicopter. That figured. Emily probably could have fallen out on her face and they would barely have noticed. She glanced down at her own comparatively diminutive chest, figuring that must be the differentiating factor.

With a sigh of resignation, Emily looked ahead and noticed Jai had gotten pretty far in front of her. He strode toward a smiling, sandy-haired man. She rushed to catch up.

"Hey! Mel. Good to see you, man." Jai greeted the man like they were old friends.

"G'day, Boofhead. How's it going?" The stranger responded with a handshake and a slap on Jai's back.

Emily frowned at him. "You two know each other?"

"Sure do. I'm sorry, Em. Let me introduce you. Emily Price, marketing maven from Madison Avenue's famed Howard & Dean Agency. Mel Townsend, Australia's best embedded-combat video man."

Emily extended her hand. "Australia? Wow. When I asked Jai if he knew any cameramen for this assignment, I didn't realize his little black book extended to another hemisphere."

Smiling, Mel shook her hand warmly. "Jai and me, we've known each other for years. Since—"

"Kandahar, two thousand and four," Jai finished for him. When he noticed Emily's surprised look, he shrugged. "I told you I've been to Afghanistan before."

She drew her brows closer together as she considered she really didn't know much about Jai at all. She'd always just assumed he'd stuck with magazine-fashion layouts with the occasional ad shoots thrown in. Hmm. Perhaps she should pay more attention.

"Onya, Jai, that's right. That was a hell of an assignment." Mel grinned.

"Mel's been embedded here in Afghanistan with the 82nd Airborne along with an Aussie reporter for the past six months. When I found out he was here on his own because the reporter he was assigned to recently shipped home, I contacted him."

"And I said bloody hell, yes, I would gladly work with this old bastard again, especially for this assignment. She's sweet. Easy peasy. Aye, Jai?"

"Compared to some of our other assignments, oh yeah," Jai agreed with a snigger but didn't elaborate.

Emily watched the interaction with interest. Definitely some history here.

"I figure any assignment where the Humvee I'm riding in doesn't get blown up is apples." Mel laughed as he addressed Emily again.

Her eyes opened wide. "Is that very often? You getting blown up, I mean?"

The ruggedly handsome Australian grinned wider. Laugh lines creased the corners of his whisky-colored eyes. "More often than I'd like. No worries, Emmie. This assignment, she'll be right. Here we'll be as safe as a joey in his mama roo's pouch."

"All righty. Good to hear." Emily nodded, wondering how she'd get through this particular assignment with this man she could barely understand. And how had her name suddenly become Emmie?

"Any word on Hawkins's ETA?" Jai asked Emily.

She shrugged. "We don't have any events scheduled for the handshake tour until tomorrow. He's supposed to arrive sometime today, but you know the military—when they do give you a timeframe, they change it ten times. I guess we have to trust the Army will get him here."

"He'll be here today." Mel nodded. "His helo should be arriving any tic of the clock now. I talked to some of the blokes in the control tower."

Emily raised a brow that Mel could get an answer so easily when all she'd gotten from the military for the past week was the runaround.

Cat Johnson

"Holy moley. Who's the stunner? She the star of this show?" Mel elbowed Jai in the side and stared in Little Miss USO's direction.

With a sideways glance at Emily, Jai nodded. "Yup. That's Kerri London herself. She and Emily are going to be good friends by the end of this tour. I can tell already."

Emily shot him a nasty look before watching the object of all the male attention make her way across the airfield in skintight red leather pants, four-inch heels and a rhinestone-studded denim jacket over her tube top. Her long red mane blew in the wind.

"Better watch it, mate. I bet this one here gets mad as a cut snake." Mel tilted his head in Emily's direction. "Fair dinkum, Emmie, she does look like she's keen to get a bit. But don't you worry. She's got nothing on you. Besides, there are more than enough diggers around here for both of you, plus some."

Emily frowned. "What's a digger?"

"Military men," Jai supplied.

She was beginning to feel as though she needed a translator, or at least an Australian/American dictionary, to speak to Mel. Even so, she got the drift of his last statement and scowled.

"I am here to work, not find men." Or diggers.

That statement was truthful. She wasn't looking for men, only for one particular man. And actually, after he'd totally ignored her last email, she wasn't all that sure she wanted that one anymore.

Emily watched the wide sway of Kerri London's shapely hips and the energetic bounce of her more-than-generous chest and sighed. This woman had all the assets Hawk would appreciate. Watching Hawk hook up with Miss Sex on Heels

140

after she'd been with him might just be more than Emily could take.

Suddenly, a warm friendly arm was around her shoulders. "Come on, love. Hot pants has her own transportation. So let's get your things and you loaded into my jeep. You keen for some tucker or a cuppa?"

Emily wasn't sure if she was keen for some tucker or not and was afraid to answer lest she commit herself to an orgy with some diggers or something. With a silent plea, she raised a brow and glanced at Jai.

"He means food and a cup of something hot to drink, Em. You'll get used to him, don't worry." Laughing out loud, Jai answered her unspoken question.

Somehow, Emily doubted that. But his offer reminded her how chilled she'd become from the helicopter ride and from standing in the wind on the airfield.

"Sure, Mel. Some food and hot coffee would be great." And getting away from Ms. Kerri *Hotpants* London even better.

"Bloody good, and then I can show you to your lush accommodations for the duration of your stay." With a wink at Jai, Mel asked, "So, Emmie, have you ever slept in a tent before?"

Emily groaned. This was going to be one heck of a trip.

"So, Grandpa. How are they still letting you fly? I'd thought you'd be back in the nursing home by now." Wally joked with the helicopter pilot. It was the same man who'd brought Hawk and the squad to their secluded camp weeks before.

Wally had explained to them all then that since he and the pilot were both from Alabama, he figured it gave him teasing rights with the old guy. So far, the elder man gave as good as he got from Wally, which never failed to amuse Hawk.

"Listen here, boy. I was flying when you weren't even a gleam in your mama's eye, and I'm still here. What does that tell you?"

"That the Army is desperate and has to hit up the senior citizen centers back in the States to recruit?" Wally shot back with a smirk.

"Ha, ha. Real funny there, kid."

The man had to be pushing sixty. He'd flown CH-46s for the Marines during the final years of the Vietnam War. The reality was that the wrinkled, gray-haired reservist was nearing the upper age limit to be allowed to fly and would soon have to retire, but the old coot was determined not to quit before they made him. For that, Hawk had to admire him.

In any case, it was nice to see any familiar face again out here, even one he'd only met once. Hawk smiled at the pilot now. "Hey, Lou. Glad to see you again."

"You too, Hawk. Didn't think I'd be picking you up again so soon. What's up? You and your two boys here giving up already? Heading for home?"

Hawk snorted out a laugh. "Not exactly." He almost wished that were the case.

"I'll tell you what, it's way better than that, Grandpa. Well, maybe not better than going home but still really great. Wait until you hear the news." His excitement evident, Wally practically bounced in his combat boots.

"Wally." Hawk growled in warning.

"What? I can tell him about my promotion, can't I?" Wally looked innocently at Hawk. A bit too innocently.

"Yes, you can tell him about your promotion." Hawk grit his teeth, willing Wally not to spill the rest of the news. The news about the recent orders that had Hawk far from happy.

It seemed Hawk's captain and his good old friend Commander Hank Miller had been busy in the weeks Hawk and his squad had been downrange. Between the two of them, and thanks to some marketing geniuses, Hawk was now part of a frigging USO handshake tour with a country singer he'd never heard of.

But that wasn't even the worst part. Thanks to a strange twist of fate, Wally's advancement had just come through from the promotions board. Someone decided it would be good press to incorporate the promotion ceremony into the tour. Of all people, now big-mouthed Wally was in on Hawk's modeling secret, and Hawk had a horrible feeling that would cost him. He'd probably have to barter his sister for Wally's secrecy.

Traveling conditions in the area were volatile enough that Hawk was instructed to take both Wally and another soldier with him. Pettit had been the no-brainer decision since he was already privy to Hawk's secret hell. Hawk had left Specialist Black from Alpha team in charge of his remaining men.

So here they were, the three amigos, heading for a frigging USO tour.

Hawk wrestled himself out of his own misery and listened as Wally told Lou his news.

"I finally made it, Grandpa. No more Specialist Trent Wallace. When you fly us back, you'll have to call me sergeant."

"You'll be lucky if I don't call you the one who accidentally fell out of the chopper." The old pilot was so amused at his own joke he laughed until he coughed so hard he had to snub out his cigarette.

As the pilot lit up another one, Hawk smiled at the single bright spot to this trip—the fact the old coot took no shit from Wally. Though Hawk feared that unless he decided to pull rank on Wally, he would certainly have to take some shit from him about this modeling gig.

Hawk considered that in under an hour he'd be with Emily again. Okay, maybe that made two bright spots in this trip. He'd get to see Emily after what seemed like a very long separation and find out if this near-physical ache he felt whenever he was alone and thinking about her was strictly a combination of sexual deprivation and the loneliness of being deployed or the real thing.

He was really hoping it was the former. This was neither the time nor the place for the real thing.

Chapter Fourteen

Taking a long sip, Emily was enjoying a nice steaming hot *cuppa* in the dining hall with Jai and her new Aussie pal when she felt his presence. Jai's wave in the direction of the door at her back confirmed her intuition. She knew without turning around Hawk had arrived.

Her heart kicked into double time. Emily didn't think that was caused by the caffeine.

"Sergeant. Glad to see you made it," Jai greeted the trio of men who strode into her sight line as one to stand next to the long table.

Emily knew the moment had come. She would have to greet Hawk, yet she still didn't know how she should act. Angry? Which she was. Indifferent? Cool and friendly like nothing had happened between them? That would require an award-winning performance on her part.

She had no clue what to do or say. Worse, she'd begun to wonder if her voice would give her away no matter what she chose to say.

Luckily for Emily, Jai made the introductions and gave her a small reprieve.

"Mel, this is our man for the shoot, Staff Sergeant Hawkins. Sergeant Hawkins, meet Mel Townsend, our video man for the next few days."

Mel rose and shook Hawk's hand. "G'day, mate."

"Sergeant Ryan Pettit and Specialist Trent Wallace." Hawk hooked a thumb at each of the two men on either side of him as he introduced them.

"Call me Wally. And after tomorrow, it'll be Sergeant instead of Specialist," one of Hawk's entourage added.

Feeling ridiculous that she had yet to speak, Emily jumped in. "I saw your captain had added the promotion ceremony to the schedule of events. Congratulations, Wally."

That earned her a wide grin from the man. Paranoid, Emily had the bad feeling Wally recognized her from the Ratskeller and was imagining how exactly his sergeant and she had spent that night in Germany.

Wally took a step closer and extended one beefy hand in her direction. "Well, hello there. And what's your name?"

Hmm. Wally was flirting with her. What exactly did that mean? He wouldn't do that if he thought she'd been with Hawk, would he?

Or would he? Especially if Hawk had told him that he was finished with her and Wally could have her next.

"Emily Price." Seething at this newest theory, Emily answered more sharply than was polite.

"Wally." The warning in Hawk's voice was evident.

"Just being friendly." Wally grinned as he took Emily's offered hand in both of his and shook it warmly. "Polite and friendly like my mama taught me."

"Your mama didn't teach you what you're thinking." Hawk took a step closer to them both and Wally dropped her hand in response. He took a step back, conceding to Hawk.

That was both interesting and maddening at the same time. Hawk hadn't made any contact with her since that one-word email right after Germany, but in true caveman fashion, he had sent a definite signal to Wally to back off immediately. He might as well have peed on her leg like a damn male dog and marked her as his territory.

Apparently he didn't want her but no one else could have her either. Lovely, but actually knowing Hawk, not that surprising.

Emily couldn't avoid it any longer. She finally looked directly into Hawk's gaze, finding it focused singly on her.

He smiled. "Hey there, Goldilocks."

The deep timbre of his voice and his small crooked smile melted her frozen heart, while at the same time reignited her anger. Particularly when Emily noted she was back to being Goldilocks again, reaffirming that any closeness they'd gained that one night in Germany had expired.

"Hi, Hawk. Glad to see you're still alive." Emily answered as flippantly as she could.

He smirked at that. "It takes a lot to kill me, doll."

Of that, she was certain, at least at those times when she was royally pissed off at him, like now. Although, during other times when she forgot to be angry, believing Hawk would be hard to kill didn't do much to ease all those ridiculously pointless nights of worrying she'd had over this man. Meanwhile, Hawk probably hadn't given her a second thought since they'd said goodbye in her hotel room in Germany.

Feeling mean, she smiled sweetly back. "Good, because I'd hate to have to start the ad campaign from scratch with a new model. So much work…" She shook her head dramatically.

Hawk laughed and Emily couldn't help but notice the adorable way crinkles appeared around his eyes. She batted away the flutter in her belly simply looking at him caused.

147

Wally raised his hand to get her attention. "I'm available to model if you need me, Ms. Price."

"No, you're not, Wally." Hawk's eyes never left her face.

Wally nodded and mouthed behind Hawk's back, "Call me."

"Nice to see you both again, Miss Price, Mr. Devereaux." Pettit, ever polite, stepped forward and shook her hand and Jai's. Then he turned to Mel. "Very nice to meet you, Mr. Townsend."

"Pleasure's mine, Sergeant." Mel pumped Pettit's hand.

The male bonding and testosterone level around the place was starting to stifle Emily.

"Well, great. Now that everyone's been introduced perhaps we should review the schedule." Emily needed something to do. She was starting to feel uncomfortable under Hawk's constant gaze.

He held up a folded piece of paper he'd had hidden somewhere in his uniform. "I've got the schedule. It's simple enough. I'll be where I'm supposed to, when I'm supposed to be there. Don't worry."

"I wasn't worried," she bit out quickly.

"No?" Hawk returned skeptically. "Good."

She hated he knew her so well even if they'd only worked together for two days. Not reviewing the schedule with all the parties involved would up her stress level considerably and Hawk darn well knew it.

Emily was considering how to suggest again they all go over the schedule together while not sounding obsessive compulsive, thereby proving Hawk right, when she noticed she was suddenly the subject of Jai's smirk and Mel's interested stare.

If she weren't careful, not only Jai, but also Mel would know about her little indiscretion with Hawk.

"Um, Jai. Don't you think we need to review the schedule with Mel?" Emily suggested.

Jai raised a brow in her direction. He had worked with her enough to know her obsessive organizational issues. Emily felt fairly certain that it was becoming increasingly obvious to Mel also. Was she that transparent to the entire male race?

"Why yes, Emily. I think it's an excellent idea to go over things with Mel. Sergeant, would you and your men like to join us while we brief our new cameraman?" Jai was humoring her. She didn't care. She had too many other issues to deal with.

Hawk nodded. "Sure. Just let us grab some chow."

"We'll be right back." Wally spoke specifically to Emily with a wink and a grin.

She couldn't help but laugh, especially when she saw Hawk set his jaw. "Okay, we'll wait for you."

Hawk, Wally and Pettit left, and when the overwhelming presence that was Hawk moved farther away, Emily could finally breathe freely for the first time in minutes.

"So, you and the Staff Sergeant, huh?" Mel grinned.

"Jai." Emily squealed the accusation, spinning to frown at him.

"What? I didn't tell him. My hand to God, Emily, I swear." Jai held up one hand in defense.

"Don't blame him, love. Fair dinkum, Emmie, Jai didn't tell me. You did. You should never play poker. You don't have the face for it."

Emily sighed. No use hiding it now.

Mel continued, "In any case, whatever happened or didn't happen doesn't matter. There sure is a good bit of tension between you two now."

"Yeah, there is." Emily laughed at Mel's huge understatement. "I just don't get how he can act like I'm his territory. Did you see him with Wally? What's up with that?"

Jai shrugged. "He's just being a man."

Mel nodded. "Right, mate. And if you use it to your advantage, Emmie, he'll play directly into your hands."

She was about to protest that maybe she didn't want him in her hands when further conversation was interrupted because Hawk and his men returned, trays of food in hand.

Changing the subject, Emily grabbed her briefcase from the floor. "Okay, let's get started."

"Super. So what have you got for me, love?" Scooting his chair closer, Mel hooked an arm around the back of Emily's chair. He ran his fingers lightly up and down her arm.

It took Emily a moment to recover from the shock of that. But after one look at his wicked grin, she realized Mel was trying to make Hawk jealous for her benefit. As petty as Emily felt, she kind of liked that idea. It would serve him right. Maybe if he had bothered to email her, things could have been different.

A glance in Hawk's direction and how his gaze remained focused on Mel's fingers still touching her told her the plan was working. It also raised another issue—what if Hawk decided to beat up Mel over what was really a sham?

She'd have to consider this carefully. On one hand, the shoot would be more difficult if the model took a swing at the cameraman. On the other hand, she loved Hawk being jealous.

She watched as Pettit and Wally attacked their food like starving men while Hawk had yet to touch his. She was certain jealousy was practically killing the man.

His face grew stonier by the second. Emily really began to fear for Mel's wellbeing. She shot a glance at Jai who looked amused by the whole turn of events. No help there.

Deciding there was nothing she could do about it now without making a scene, she ignored Mel and his wandering fingers, refused to look at Hawk and his possessive anger and took out her papers to review the schedule with all involved.

When all else failed, resort to work mode. That was Emily's usual modus operandi in times of personal crisis, and she saw no need to change it now.

She focused solely on the paper in front of her. "Okay. First thing after breakfast with the troops tomorrow morning is Wally's promotion ceremony with Hawk and Kerri London."

Hawk would surely need dental work by the time he left Bagram. Since he'd arrived, he'd kept his jaw clenched in an attempt to not tell that damn Aussie to get his fucking hands off Emily.

The cameraman had been all handy with her at dinner, then even worse the next morning. The bastard had the nerve to kiss her cheek at breakfast, leaving Hawk to wonder precisely where he'd spent the night.

Exactly how long had Emily and Crocodile Dundee been here in Bagram together? Hawk didn't know, but he sure as hell wanted to find out.

In spite of their history together, or maybe because of it, Hawk would never take Emily as the kind who would sleep around with a guy she'd just met. He knew he'd been the exception in Germany, not the rule. But damn, with this guy anything was possible.

She might see the Aussie as different. Smooth-talking foreigners were sexy. Not that Hawk could judge that kind of shit in other men, but chicks always dug guys with foreign accents.

The possibility of Emily being with this Mel Townsend character was all Hawk could think about. And now he had to participate in Wally's promotion ceremony in front of a hundred and fifty, maybe two hundred soldiers and act like nothing was wrong. They were all gathered there not for him or for Wally's promotion, but instead to get a look at this supposedly famous singer.

Wally leaned closer. "I can't believe Kerri London is going to help promote me."

"You've heard of her?" Hawk looked at Wally, surprised.

"Hell, yeah. You haven't? Oh, come on, Hawk. You've heard her songs. I'm sure of it. 'Red Lipstick and a New Pair of Shoes'?"

Hawk raised a brow. "Must have missed that one."

"'Only Your Dog Loves You Now'?" Wally threw out another song title, or at least what Hawk assumed was a song.

He laughed. "Nope. Sorry. But that sounds like a good one."

Wally let out a frustrated sigh. "What do you listen to?"

"Your bitching, mostly." Hawk grinned until the superior officer who'd be promoting Wally climbed the stairs. He and Wally both stood at attention.

The red-lipstick-wearing star herself preceded the officer onto the makeshift wooden stage. At least they'd put her in a flak jacket. Perhaps with her covered up a bit, Wally would be able to avoid drooling on her during the ceremony.

Model Soldier

"Attention to orders!" The sound reverberated through the crowd. In unison, the gathering of soldiers on the ground in front of the stage snapped firmly to attention.

A few hundred men in formation, all in their ACUs looking sharp and professional—Hawk knew that sight would make Emily happy for her shot. He located her blonde head and cute figure quickly in the crowd. Then he found that bastard cameraman near her and scowled.

Hawk forced down the anger and made himself pay attention as the ceremony began and the officer read the promotion warrant.

"The Secretary of the Army has reposed special trust and confidence in the patriotism, valor, fidelity and professional excellence of Trent Shirley Wallace..."

Shirley? Oh, Wally was never going to hear the end of that. Hawk had to control his grin. He had renewed faith in Wally's discretion regarding the modeling assignment now that Hawk had something equally embarrassing on him.

As the reading of the warrant continued and finally came to a conclusion, Hawk had to bite the inside of his cheek to keep from laughing at the expression of horror on Wally's face at the public exposure of his middle name.

"In view of these qualities and his demonstrated leadership potential and dedicated service to the US Army, he is therefore promoted from specialist to sergeant."

For the final piece of the promotion, the officer who'd read the warrant whispered instructions to the singer, who, to Wally's great pleasure Hawk was certain, personally pinned his new stripes onto his uniform.

"Congratulations, Sergeant Wallace," she cooed to the accompaniment of a few camera flashes and the collective cheer of the assembly.

The promotion part of this gig was over, but unfortunately Hawk's job was far from done. Next came the picture-taking part of the program. Every one of those many soldiers standing out in the cold was here not for Wally or Hawk, but rather to get his picture taken with Kerri London. Hawk was supposed to stand next to her for each and every shot whether they wanted him there or not.

"Hey there, sugar. Sorry we didn't get to meet earlier. I'm Kerri."

Hawk glanced down at her now as she addressed him directly. He shook her extended hand. "I'm Staff Sergeant David Hawkins."

Kerri raised one thin eyebrow and smiled seductively. "That's a mouthful, darlin', although I'm sure you are just that. What should I call you?"

Hawk raised a brow of his own. "You can call me Hawk."

"Mmm. I like that. Hawk. Nice." She'd said his name as if she was trying out the feel of it on her tongue before turning toward Wally. "Now, Sergeant Trent Shirley Wallace. Since you're the man of the hour, you get your picture made first."

She flashed a smile at Wally, who visibly melted beneath her gaze.

"Shirley's a family name, ma'am. My mama's maiden name. We take family seriously where I'm from." Wally pressed so close to Kerri for the pose they looked glued at the hip.

"A fine man such as yourself, I'm sure you do take family serious, sugar. Now smile pretty for the camera."

Rasta-photographer motioned for Hawk to step closer to her. He did, though leaving a good six inches between his leg and hers. The Army photographer the USO had brought in for this tour stood next to Rasta and snapped away. Hawk's damn face was going to be everywhere. He sighed at the thought.

The snap of the camera heralded one picture down, two hundred or so more to go.

Actually, the entire process took less time than Hawk anticipated. He thought they'd be there until dinner considering Kerri took the time to personally flirt with each and every one of the men who climbed the stairs to stand next to her for a picture. All under the watchful eye of her bodyguard of course.

By the end, if Hawk never heard the words *sugar* or *smile* again, it would be too soon.

When the long line of soldiers finally disappeared and Kerri and Hawk were left alone on stage with no one but the photographer, the woman still amazingly had the capacity to smile at him.

"Well, thank you, Hawk. It was nice to have company for this one. I'm usually alone."

He somehow doubted Ms. Kerri London was ever alone unless she wanted to be.

Hawk had to laugh. "We both know not one of those soldiers was here to have their picture taken with me. They're probably cutting me out of the prints with their knives as we speak."

She laughed and smacked his chest playfully. "You're a funny one. But I can tell you I wouldn't be throwing your photo away. I bet just your picture could keep a girl warm at night."

Shaking his head at her with a slightly embarrassed grin, Hawk broke eye contact with Kerri and noticed Emily next to the stage. She was telling Rasta-photographer and Crocodile Dundee something, but judging from the look on her face as she noticed Kerri touching him, she was pissed.

Wasn't that interesting...

Not one to look a gift horse in the mouth, Hawk played right into her jealousy. "Then maybe we should have the photographer snap a shot of just the two of us. One copy for you and one for me. What do you say, Ms. London?"

"I'd love that, sugar. But only if you call me Kerri."

"You got it, Kerri." From the corner of his eye he watched Emily's face redden.

He draped one arm around the star, and for the first one of all those many, many pictures, Hawk actually smiled.

Life was short. Hawk had learned that from watching too many lives end too soon. He wasn't one to waste it. He also wasn't usually one to play games, but sometimes, such as now, it might be necessary.

Emily may be pissed, she may even be sleeping with the Aussie, but he knew one thing for certain, he wouldn't give up easily the second chance he'd been handed to be with her. They'd been thrown together again for this USO thing by fate or luck or frigging Dalton for all he knew. But whoever or whatever had put them together, Hawk wouldn't waste the opportunity.

Disengaging from Kerri, Hawk turned toward a seething Emily. "Okay, boss. What's next on the agenda?"

He knew exactly what was on the schedule. It was a tour of the base facilities, but he wanted Emily to have to talk to him.

Emily shot him a withering look that might wilt a less determined man. "I don't know. Ask Jai."

Hawk hid his smile. She knew. She had that schedule memorized, just like he did. She was just too mad to answer him. Yup, this jealousy thing just might work to his advantage.

Loud enough so she would hear, Hawk said, "Come on, Kerri. Off to our next stop." He extended his hand to help the singer down the steps just as Emily turned in a huff and stalked away.

Hawk watched her go and grinned. He always did enjoy a challenge. If nothing else, winning a fuming Emily back from the Aussie would be that.

"Bring it on."

"You say something, Hawk?" Kerri was nearer to him than he'd realized.

"Hmm? Oh, sorry. I'm just talking to myself. Bad habit I picked up from being deployed so much. You ready for our tour?"

"Ready and willing, sugar." She winked and extended her arm for him to take.

Strolling arm in arm with her, like the gentleman he sometimes pretended to be, Hawk shook his head at himself. In the not-so-distant past, this woman would have been right up his alley. A hot and willing redhead, a pre-set and definite date of departure, deployment as the ideal excuse to not call her again... The perfect set-up for a short-lived hot-and-heavy fling, and Hawk wasn't at all interested.

He had to wonder about why he had this sudden change of heart or at least taste in women. Then he glanced up and saw Emily's irate, quick stride ahead of them and Hawk figured he already knew.

Chapter Fifteen

Emily stared down at her copy of the schedule on the desk. One more day for a few more staged photo ops and then back to New York.

She wasn't sure if she was happy to get away from having to watch Hawk with that harpy or not. After this tour was over, she'd likely never see the man again. Even as angry as she was, that thought hurt.

"I told you before. You keep frowning like that and you're gonna get wrinkles."

His deep, achingly familiar voice suddenly filled the room. She cursed herself for leaving the door to the office open so he could sneak up on her.

Hawk stepped inside and swung that door closed. He strode directly to stand behind her chair. He leaned down and planted a hand on the desk on each side of her. She was caged by his massive forearms.

"I thought we'd never be alone." Hawk spoke so close to Emily's ear, she could feel the warm heat of his breath on her skin. His close proximity sent a shiver straight down her spine, which only made her frown deeper.

They were alone in the USO office she'd been allowed to use, and this late at night there wasn't much chance of that changing. She wasn't sure she wanted to be alone with this man. It was too tempting. Even as angry as she was that he hadn't emailed, that he'd spent the day on Kerri's arm, she knew she wouldn't be able to control herself. She'd give him anything he wanted. She absolutely hated giving him that satisfaction.

Hawk sidled up closer behind her until she felt the hard muscles of his thighs pressed against her back. Running his hands up both her arms, he bent and kissed her neck lightly.

"What do you think you're doing?" She pushed the chair away from the desk, stood and spun to face him. He stepped back to let her, then shoved her discarded chair aside and moved in again.

With one warm, rough hand, he cupped her face. Her butt was pressed against the desk. She had nowhere to go to get away from him. Did she really want to get away? She had to swallow the lump forming in her throat as she ached to reach out and touch the man so close to her.

"I'm picking up where we left off in Germany." His gaze focused on her mouth as he bent slowly toward her.

As much as her lips craved his, Emily's eyes flew open wide at the nerve of that statement. "Oh no, you're not."

"Why not? You want me as much as I want you. I can see it written all over your face."

"That's not true." Emily was one of the worst liars on earth, but she figured it was worth a shot.

Hawk grinned. "You've said that before, beautiful. Remember back in Germany right before you jumped me?"

The reminder fought back Emily's raging hormones and brought her screeching to her senses. "You're right. I did, and you never even emailed me afterward. Oh, wait, sorry. Correction. You did email me. One damn word and then nothing. And now you're all flirty with that Kerri London."

She shoved him away hard, but a part of her immediately regretted the loss of his warmth.

Hawk narrowed his eyes, and for the first time during this encounter, he appeared unsure of himself. "No flirtier than you are with that Aussie cameraman."

"I am not."

"Bullshit."

"It is not bullshit. I do not flirt with him." Emily feared she might have actually stomped one foot like a child as she made that statement, but continued anyway. "You want to see flirting, take a look at Kerri London. That is flirting. I do not flirt."

"Okay, maybe you don't, but Crocodile Mel sure as hell does with you, and you are all too ready to let him, aren't you?"

"So what? I'm not involved with anyone. You have no claim on me, David Hawkins."

"No, I don't. You're right." Impossibly, he looked almost sad about that. Hawk drew in a long, slow breath. "I'm sorry I didn't email you."

An apology from Hawk. Emily had to wonder exactly how many women could claim they'd received one of those. She guessed not many.

"Why didn't you?"

He let out a short laugh. "It seemed like a good idea at the time."

Emily crossed her arms and glared at him. "Yeah, well it wasn't. In fact, I can tell you it sucked."

Don't cry, don't cry, don't cry. Emily repeated the mantra to herself. Willing her misty eyes to listen up and follow orders, she stared unfocused at the stained ceiling.

"I know. It was a mistake and I really am sorry." Hawk moved closer. She didn't move away.

"Why are you bothering kissing up to me? Little Miss USO was all over you today. Why don't you go be with her? I'm fairly certain you'll get lucky." *If you haven't already.*

Hawk chuckled. "Little Miss USO. That's funny. And I'm not interested in Kerri. I'm interested in you."

Hating the hope that was beginning to sprout in her chest, she held on to the memory of a smiling Hawk attached to Kerri London's hip all day. She hated it about as much as she loathed that he called her Kerri while Emily had been everything from doll to Goldilocks to boss on this trip. Yet Hawk still claimed he was interested in her.

Emily let out a huff of air. "You don't show it very well."

"I'll show you now." Hawk's lips covered hers in an instant.

She couldn't fight it. Truth be told, she didn't try. As his mouth crushed hers, the tears escaped until they wet her face and crept into the kiss.

"I'm so sorry, Emily." Hawk wiped her cheek as he continued to deliver kisses between his words. "So sorry."

He lifted her like she weighed no more than a rag doll, set her on the desk's edge and stepped between her legs. His kisses became more passion-filled and less apologetic.

Emily knew being with him again now would make leaving again in two days even harder than it had been the first time they parted in Germany. She hated that she didn't seem to care. She wanted to be with him, as painful as it would be later.

Hawk pulled back and grabbed her face in both of his hands. "I'm gonna lock the door."

He stared at her, waiting.

"Okay." With a tremor in her voice, Emily answered the question he hadn't asked.

Drawing in a sharp breath, Hawk spun away. He flipped the lock and was back in the blink of an eye. Then his hands were everywhere, pulling at her clothes. Emily didn't blame Hawk for his haste. Her hands were on him too. She couldn't get enough of him.

Simply touching wasn't enough, even after he'd undone her pants and slid his hand inside her panties to find her clit. She wanted his hot skin pressed against hers. Wanted him inside her. That would be the only thing that might satisfy her need. Even then, she wouldn't stay satisfied for very long. This man haunted her.

Wasn't that always the way? The man she couldn't have was of course the one she wanted.

He pressed her back so she lay against the desk with her feet hanging off the edge. His gaze followed his hands down her body as he pushed her trousers down her legs.

"Emily." He swallowed hard. There was a question evident in both his expression and his voice as he said her name—her real name.

In answer, she spread her legs and made room for him to step between them. He drew in a shuttering breath and reached for his back pocket.

Hawk covered himself with the condom he'd pulled out. Why did he have it? For her? For Kerri? Was it part of every GI's standard equipment?

She didn't find answers to her questions before he leaned over her. His gaze boring into hers, Hawk slid deeply inside her. He was with her, not with Kerri. That had to mean something.

The feel of him was so familiar, even here and now on a cold metal desk in a strange office in the middle of Afghanistan. With Hawk over her, loving her, Emily felt like she was home.

The delicate wall she'd worked so hard to construct around her bruised heart crumbled more with every thrust of Hawk's body into hers. She responded to him like they'd been made for each other...and in two days she'd leave him again.

Emily realized she was in big trouble when she found herself crying and coming at the same time. Her body clenched around him as the tears flowed freely.

More tenderly than a man his size and usual demeanor should have been capable of, Hawk wrapped her in his arms. He shushed her to quiet her sobs while still making love to her. With a shudder and a groan, he came a moment after her.

Still covering her body with his, he held her tighter. "You all right?"

"No." That was the truth, plain and simple.

"I am sorry." Hawk brushed a stray hair out of her face. The act nearly melted her. She couldn't let it. He was who he was—a love-them-and-leave-them soldier whose life was the Army. A moment of gentleness didn't alter that.

"I know you are. But nothing's changed. You're going to do it again. Ignore me."

"No, I won't."

Staring up at the ceiling, Emily let out a bitter laugh. "Yes, you will. You'll go away in two days and I'll never hear from you again unless you're forced into another assignment."

"You will hear from me. You'll see." The determination in his voice almost made her believe him.

With two muscular arms, Hawk levered himself off both her and the desk. With a snap of latex, he tugged off the used condom and pushed it deep into the trashcan. After the evidence was buried beneath the discarded papers and what looked like the remnants of someone's meal, he began to button his pants. With a sigh, she sat up and started to do the same.

His eyes never left her as she dressed. "Damn. I wish I could take you back to my tent with me."

Emily wished the same thing. If she was going to have a freshly broken heart, she might as well enjoy a full night of sex first. "We could go to my tent maybe?"

Reaching out to touch her face, he shook his head with a sad smile. "That would be very nice, but it's not a good idea. I could get in big trouble. Being in here was too damn risky as it was."

"Okay, I understand." Not really, but...

Hawk stepped forward and drew her close. He bent low and kissed her again. He let out a sound of near pain when he pulled away. "Ready to get back to the real world?"

Not even close.

Still trembling, Emily nodded. "Sure."

Hawk looked them both over one last time, she guessed to make sure they were dressed and put back together enough to be seen in public. Then he moved toward the door.

He paused with his hand on the lock. "I'll walk you to your tent. You shouldn't be out alone this late."

Nodding, she grabbed the folder from the desk and pretended they hadn't just had sex on top of it as she followed him out the door.

Making love to Emily was easy. Trying to get some sleep afterward knowing she was here on base so close and yet so far—not so much.

Tired and still wanting more of her, Hawk finally dragged his sorry ass out of his rack and hit the showers. The hot water striking his back felt good. He had plans to stay in there for a long time. Or at least until he felt human again.

While he stood and let the water wash away the fatigue, his mind wandered back to his too-short time with Emily. His body reacted with some pretty visible results. He considered if he had the energy or the desire to deal with it now.

"Hawk! Are you in here?" Pettit's voice so close on the other side of the shower curtain deflated Hawk's erection in no time.

"Yeah. What?" Hawk knew he sounded as exhausted and cranky as he felt. A man couldn't even take a damn shower in peace. He'd deal with this kind of shit at the FOB where attacks came day and night, but here during a damn USO tour he should be able to relax for five minutes in the shower.

"Holy shit, Hawk. You have to get out here."

Apparently there'd be no relaxing and no more shower.

Soap still in his eyes, Hawk turned off the water and quickly wrapped a towel around his waist, not worried any longer he'd embarrass himself with an Emily-induced hard-on.

Ready for anything but really wishing he had his gun and some clothes on, Hawk pushed out from behind the shower curtain. He came face to face with a very flustered-looking Pettit.

"What? What's wrong?"

"It's Wally."

Oh no. When it came to attracting trouble, that kid was a life-sized magnet.

"Where is he?" Hawk pulled his uniform T-shirt over his head, not taking the time to tuck the hem into the waistband of his pants.

"That's the part you aren't going to believe. He's in Kerri's tent."

"Aw, fuck." Hawk jumped on one foot as he shoved a sockless foot into his boot, grabbed his jacket in his fist and ran for the door.

He'd had a bad feeling about Wally's ability to resist that woman's overt flirting. What he'd been counting on was that Kerri was all show and she wouldn't actually follow through.

Bad call on Hawk's part, because now Wally could get into huge trouble. Looking down at his barely dressed, definitely non-regulation appearance, Hawk realized so could he if anyone saw him looking like this. Hell of a poster boy for the US Army he'd turned out to be.

Hawk barely noticed the cold air against his still-wet skin as they ran through the entrance to the tent used by Kerri's entourage...only to be stopped by the steel wall that was her personal bodyguard.

He heard Kerri say, "Let them through, Tony. It's okay."

Looking around the man, Hawk saw Kerri, fully clothed and wringing her hands. "I didn't know who else to call. I'm pretty sure he can get into trouble for this, and I didn't want to do that. I had Tony look for you but he could only find Ryan."

Hawk looked around the otherwise empty space and frowned. "I don't understand. Where's Wally and what happened?"

Kerri hooked a thumb at the door behind her. "In there."

That didn't explain much, but Hawk didn't require words when he could just go find out for himself. He preferred that actually—seeing things for himself.

Striding to the next room, the picture awaiting him there truly was worth a thousand words.

"Jesus, Wally."

Seeing his newly promoted sergeant stretched out face down, naked and tangled up with an equally undressed female had Hawk cursing even more colorfully beneath his breath.

Judging by the woman's uniform lying on the floor, she was with the 455th Air Expeditionary Wing of the USAF. Fraternization at its most blatant.

"Pettit, get in here. Kerri, can your guard keep everyone out of here until I clean up this mess. I mean everybody. I don't care if it's a five-star general or the president of the United States, they cannot, I repeat cannot enter this room."

"You got it, Hawk. Tony?" Kerri glanced back at her hired brute as he folded his arms and nodded, relieving Hawk's worries somewhat on that front.

Now for Wally... The scene looked like a cross between a frat-house party and a Roman orgy. The violation was enough to get Wally court-marshaled and kicked out of the service.

Hawk eyed an empty bottle of bourbon lying sideways on the floor. At least that helped to explain things.

He picked up the glass bottle and handed it to Kerri. "Civilians can probably get away with drinking on base, but Wally..." He shook his head.

Kerri got his drift and nodded, eyeing the bottle. "Gotcha. I'll be more careful with my empty Wild Turkey bottles in the future."

Stashing it deep in the garbage bin already mostly filled with water bottles and Styrofoam plates, Kerri winked at him, and Hawk said a silent thank you that she was being so cool about this. They might just get Wally out of this mess without a trip to the brig first.

"We've got to get him up, dressed and out of here." Hawk had been thinking out loud, but Pettit stepped forward as if he'd issued an order.

Pettit grabbed a bottle of water off the floor and cracked the top. Standing over the bed, he looked a bit too pleased as he doused Wally's head with the entire contents.

It took a bit of time to bring Wally to. He started out sputtering and then looked hazily around the room through squinted eyes. Hawk watched as the pieces began to fall into place in Wally's addled brain. He waited for full realization to set in before he bothered yelling at him.

Wally glanced down at the naked girl beneath him and there it was—the oh-shit look.

"Wally, what the hell were you thinking?" Hawk crossed his arms and waited.

Still naked, Wally sat up on the edge of the bunk. He looked dazed as he shook his head. "Hell if I know. I guess I wasn't thinking."

"Obviously." Hawk averted his eyes with a scowl. "Can you please put some clothes on?"

Wally grabbed a pair of underwear off the ground from amid the tangle of discarded clothes, pulled them on and then sat down heavily on the edge of the bed with his forearms braced on his knees.

Airman whatever-her-name-was still didn't stir, which was probably for the better. One problem at a time.

"Oh, he was thinking all right, Hawk, but with the little head instead of the big one." Pettit grinned at his own joke.

Hawk shot him a look to silence him before he turned his attention back to Wally. "If someone besides me and Pettit found you here, you could at the very least be stripped of your new rank. You'd be damn lucky if you didn't end up out of the Army totally with a dishonorable discharge."

"I know, Hawk. I was stupid."

Hawk continued, undeterred by Wally's contrition. "And then we have to hope she doesn't press charges. You outrank her. If she decides to cry sexual harassment or worse, rape—"

"I know. I'm sorry. I swear to you. I won't let it happen again. Ever." Wally shook his head miserably.

Hawk went on, "And if she does end up talking and you lose that promotion and get busted back down to specialist or lower, you know it's going to fuck with your head. I can't, I won't, have you become a liability downrange and put my men at risk, Wally."

Wally simply sat looking repentant, head shaking. Hands shaking too, now that Hawk took a closer glance.

Hawk sighed. "Get dressed and get out of here."

"Yes, sir." Judging by his tone and the sudden switch to the formal *sir*, Wally had realized he was in very deep shit.

Once dressed, an obviously hungover Wally slunk out of the tent after taking one last backward glance at the unconscious girl still on the bed.

Pettit watched him go. "You think he learned his lesson?"

Hawk laughed bitterly. "No."

"But I bet he'll at least be on his best behavior for the rest of the time we're here," Pettit offered.

Hawk sighed. "Yeah, maybe. But I can tell you one thing. I'm not going to let him forget this. When it comes time for maintenance duty back at camp, Sergeant Wallace, if he's lucky enough to still hold that title, is going to be first on my list."

Pettit laughed. "I have no doubt, Hawk. I have no doubt."

Grabbing a twisted sheet hanging from the bottom of the bed, Hawk pulled it up, covering the naked girl the best he could without getting too close.

"What do we do with her?" Pettit asked with a glance at the Airman.

Good question.

"I guess we leave her here to sleep it off. Will you go make sure Wally keeps himself out of sight until he doesn't look and smell like he rolled in a bottle of bourbon?"

"Sure thing, Hawk." With a nod, Pettit left to do as he was told like a good soldier. If only Wally could be so obedient.

Turning, Hawk noticed Kerri hovering in the doorway. "That okay with you? If we leave her here to sleep it off?"

"Of course, it's her room while I'm here anyway. Until now she's been no problem. Real quiet girl." Kerri glanced at the figure on the bed then looked back to Hawk. "She did hint her boyfriend back home had sent her a Dear John, or I guess Dear Jane letter. That's probably what got into her, besides Wally that is." Kerri laughed at her own little joke and walked out to the front of the tent.

Hawk followed her. "Thanks for calling me. It could save his career."

Kerri smiled. "No problem."

Hawk and Emily had broken some rules themselves last night. He smothered any feelings of guilt about yelling at Wally. Yeah, Hawk had made an unwise decision, but with one big difference—Emily was a civilian, making it a shade less illegal. They also hadn't been drunk. Nope. Alcohol wasn't required for either of them to want to jump each other at inappropriate times and places.

Hawk glanced back at the doorway to the room where the Airman still slept. "I just hope she's smart about this."

"She's a decent kid, Hawk. She's been assigned to me as kind of a liaison since I arrived. I think she'll do the right thing and keep this quiet. She will if I have anything to say about it anyway."

Hawk smiled. "You're one in a million, Kerri."

She nodded. "Yeah, I know, Hawk. Too bad I'm not the one in a million for you."

Surprised, Hawk had to laugh. "You don't want a tired, mean old soldier like me, Kerri. Believe me."

"You'd be surprised what I might want." Kerri ran one red polished nail down Hawk's T-shirt.

It did nothing for him. Sure, she was hot. Yeah, a few months ago he may have fallen into bed right there with this woman, broken a few rules and never looked back. But things had changed and without his even realizing it.

Hawk grabbed her hand, moved her fingers from his chest and gave them a gentle squeeze. "Sorry, Kerri."

She smiled. "Whoever she is, I hope she appreciates you."

Laughing out loud, Hawk shook his head. "Nope. I can honestly say she doesn't. Not yet anyway. But one day, she will."

"She better. If she doesn't, give me a call. Now that this little situation has bonded you with my bodyguard, Tony, your phone call might actually make it through to me."

Hawk smiled. "I'll keep that in mind. Thanks again."

"No problem, sugar."

He pulled on the jacket he still held balled in one fist. With socks shoved in one pocket and his shirt still not tucked properly into his pants or his pants tucked into his boots, Hawk

171

Cat Johnson

took a quick peek outside the door. Making sure no brass was around to see him, he skirted around the side of Kerri's tent and headed for his own.

Chapter Sixteen

Wally's poor judgment and the still-looming possible consequences aside, Hawk still walked to the USO offices with a spring in his step. He may have more events with Kerri, the ever-present Tony and the mismatched team of photographers for another day's fun, but he also had another entire day with Emily. If he had anything to say about it, they'd also have some more private time together tonight.

He opened the door to the office and realized by the look of the full room he was the last to enter. Used to being the first to arrive most places, Hawk decided to cut himself some slack. His morning had already been fairly eventful and the day hadn't even really started yet.

Kerri, sporting an interesting outfit comprised of a camo flak jacket and black high-heel boots, was the first to greet him. "Good morning again, sugar."

"Morning." His gaze searched the room as he responded to Kerri.

Spotting Emily, Hawk started to go over when Kerri stopped him with a hand on his arm.

"Oh, Hawk. That issue you were worried about? It won't be a problem. She is so embarrassed she made me swear that I wouldn't tell anyone about it, so I think your boy is in the clear."

That got his full attention. Hawk let out a breath filled with relief. "Thanks, Kerri. That's really good to hear."

"Yeah, I thought you'd like that." Kerri grinned and then went back to sipping from her water bottle.

Hawk glanced across the room to Emily. She sat at the corner desk scribbling furiously with her head down. Happy to find her separated from the group so they'd have some privacy, Hawk went to her. He smiled at the memories that flooded him as he passed what had become *their* desk the evening before.

"Hey, sweet thing. I missed you last night." He lowered his voice so the rest of the room's inhabitants wouldn't hear.

She raised her head and venom shot from her glare. "Don't you talk to me. Jai will be running things today as soon as I give him some instructions. Don't worry, Hawk. You won't have to see me again before you leave."

"What? Why? What's the matter?" Hawk frowned, totally and completely confused. He tried to catch her eye, to read her face, but she looked away. "Emily. Look at me."

Standing, she started toward the door. He grasped her arm. "Emily. What's the matter? Everything seemed fine last night. I thought—"

"I saw you," she hissed.

Hawk frowned. "Saw me what?"

She didn't answer, but he saw her eyes grow glassy with unshed tears combined with anger.

"Emily, you saw what?" He began again just as a deafening blast rocked the ground they stood upon. It was so strong he had to reach out with his free hand and grab the desk to steady himself.

"What in the bloody hell was that?" After that exclamation, the Aussie was running out the office door, video camera in hand, straight toward the undisclosed danger rather than away from it like any sane civilian would.

"Wait. Don't..." Hawk yelled to stop the idiot, but he was gone already.

Emily took that opportunity to wiggle from his loosened grip on her arm and make a run for the door herself.

"Emily, no!" Hawk didn't know what had exploded, but he did know he wanted Emily near him where he could protect her until he found out.

He tackled her just as she cleared the entrance of the building, taking them both down into the dirt as the many sirens scattered throughout the base erupted. Amid the garbled loudspeaker announcements, people were running everywhere he looked.

"Get off of me." Nearly hysterical, she struggled against him, unbelievably strong for a female her size.

His attention split between the bedlam on base and the hellion beneath him, Hawk somehow managed to grab both of Emily's flailing fists in one of his hands and pin them above her head.

"Listen to me. I don't know what the hell is wrong with you I don't have time to deal with it now. I'm a little busy trying to keep you alive. Now get the fuck back in that building or I'll put you in there myself."

He hated treating her like this, resorting to frightening her, but it was necessary. Emily stared at him with a mix of hate and fear in her tear-filled eyes. Finally, she nodded and looked calm enough he felt confident he could let her up and she wouldn't bolt.

Back in the USO office, Hawk had no time to comfort Emily because chaos had broken out among their small group. Hawk released his grip on her arm once she was safely inside. He stood stunned, deciding how to deal with this situation, just as the Aussie returned to the room.

"The east wall of the prison facility is blown to bloody bits," the breathless cameraman reported.

Hawk instinctively reached for his M16 and realized it wasn't there. All he had was a damn pistol. It was better than nothing, but damn, he'd give anything for Pettit and Wally right about now, and his automatic weapon.

"Look here, mates." Mel stood in the center of the room and addressed the group. "We're sitting ducks if they find us here in this office with nothing but Hawkins's pistol to protect six people. I think we should make a run for it. There's a bunker not far—"

Tony shook his head, pivoting it emphatically atop his abnormally thick neck. "No way. We stay here where I can protect Kerri."

"How far is that bunker?" Jai asked over Tony.

Hawk looked at the group—Emily an emotional mess, Kerri in spike heels, the three-hundred-pound Tony who probably hadn't run anywhere since grade-school gym class, the unarmed Aussie ready to take on the insurgents single-handedly and one Rastafarian with a camera. The answer to the bunker question was obvious to Hawk—not close enough to risk it.

Knowing he had to do something to manage the situation and fast before things spiraled any more out of control, he shouted, "Listen up!"

When the room fell silent, he continued. "When we're taking pictures or up on stage, you all can be in charge. But here and now, for this situation, if you people want to stay alive and get out of here in one piece, I'm in charge. That means you do what I say quickly, calmly and without question. Do you understand?"

He looked around the room and saw a collective nod from among the assembly. The combined adrenaline felt almost palpable to Hawk's over-tuned senses.

"Now, here's what we know. Someone, most likely a guerilla faction of the Taliban, blew the wall of the base prison. I assume they did that to break out someone important to them who's being held there, and until they accomplish that goal they aren't going to leave."

"And for some even more good news," Mel piped in, "that facility with the giant hole in the wall can hold up to five hundred prisoners. Most of them Taliban or al Qaeda suspects who are not bloody happy to be there."

Great. Hawk sighed.

"But won't they just want to get the hell out of prison and run for the hills?" Kerri asked.

Mel shook his head. "We have to remember, love. These people don't care if they live or die, and they will gladly take us with them. In their opinion, the more evil occupiers—meaning us—they can kill the better."

Hawk took back control of the floor before this guy frightened them into further frenzy. "We have an undisclosed number of insurgents within the perimeter of the base who are obviously in possession of explosives and most likely weapons. We have the escaped prisoners, and I'm assuming snipers outside the fences. But we're within the largest US base in Afghanistan. The troops here are well armed and trained. They can handle this."

"So what does this all mean for us, Hawk? What do we do? Tell us what to do, sugar." Kerri's unquestioning faith in him put even more pressure on the already overwhelming situation.

Hawk had been prepared for almost every scenario in training and in battle, but he was experienced in leading a squad of skilled professional soldiers, not a laughably diverse group of untrained civilians.

"We stay here and sit tight for now." He didn't want to say it, but he didn't know what else to do without putting them all in jeopardy. At least he had some semblance of control here. If the insurgents came through the door, he had his pistol. He knew Tony had some firepower hidden on his person too. That made two pistols to at least defend the women with.

If their attackers chose to blow the building instead... Hawk decided not to think about that right now. He could only hope the baddies were more occupied with freeing the prisoners— possibly five hundred of them if the facility was at full capacity. Shit. How the fuck did this happen?

Maybe he should risk a run for the bunker with them all.

Catching Emily's gaze, he saw hate and anger in her eyes before she looked away again. One problem at a time. He couldn't figure out what was wrong with her if he didn't keep her alive first.

"If only we had some weapons." Jai let out a breath.

Hawk shook his head to disagree. "No. Weapons in the hands of the untrained are worse than no weapons at all."

"Four years ROTC in college. One tour in the sandbox courtesy of the Army and two more years embedded as an AP photographer in Kandahar. That enough training for you?" Jai cocked one brow in his direction.

Well, damn. That's what he got for judging a book by its cover. Hawk nodded. "Yeah, it's enough, but we still don't have any weapons."

"I have a weapon, and I know how to use it," Tony said succinctly.

178

Just as Hawk had suspected. How Tony had smuggled that on base Hawk didn't even want to imagine.

"I know, Tony, and I'm glad for that at least. But whatever you're hiding not so effectively in that shoulder-holster under your jacket doesn't have enough range or firepower to do us much good against what those guys have out there."

"I have a phone." Emily spoke for the first time since the explosion.

"You have signal? I haven't been able to get shit out here." Tony held up his own phone.

"Satellite phone," Jai answered Tony's question for Emily.

This whole thing was too surreal, discussing cell-phone signal in the middle of an attack on a supposedly secure base.

Hawk laughed. "Well, that's great. Who are you gonna call, Emily?"

"My boss." She answered him with unmistakable attitude.

She was being deliberately evasive because she was angry with him, for what he would love to know.

"Emily. Please. This is not the time—"

"My boss is engaged to BB Dalton. He's part of a SpecOps team." Emily interrupted his lecture.

Yeah, Hawk knew the team. "Emily, Dalton and his boys are too far away to do us any good. From the States or even Germany to here is—"

She shook her head violently. "No, they're not home. Katie mentioned they're at some training thing in Kabul this week. That's not too far."

Hawk could have hugged her for that piece of information, if he thought she wouldn't slug him. He laughed. "No, that's not too far."

Hawk never thought he'd be happy to hear the name Dalton again, but in this situation he was.

Kabul to Bagram was probably about sixty kilometers. If Zeta could lay hands on a Black Hawk, which Hawk had no doubt they could, they could be there in under thirty minutes. But then what? Seven men against an insurgent uprising and prison break. Even Zeta might have trouble with those odds.

"Call her, Em. Call now," Jai said.

Emily fumbled getting the phone out of her bag. She dialed with visibly shaking hands. After a few tense moments her expression became visibly relieved. "Katie. I need you to get a hold of BB right away…"

The entire process probably took less than five minutes but moved in slow motion the way things often did in times of crisis. It seemed like an eternity between the time Emily had told her boss about the situation and disconnected, and when her phone rang again.

The attention of every person in the room was on her as she fumbled to pick it up.

"Hello. BB, thank God." Emily's voice broke on a sob.

Hawk moved to stand closer to Emily. Tears glistening in her eyes, she spoke with Dalton through the satellite phone. She nodded a few times at whatever he'd said, then she held the phone up to Hawk. "He wants to talk to you."

Taking a deep, steadying breath, Hawk pressed the phone to his ear. "Dalton, it's Hawk."

"Hawkins, am I glad you're there with Emily for this."

"Me too." More than Dalton could ever know.

The connection was bad and Dalton sounded as if he was shouting over a hell of a lot of background noise, but Hawk was happy to hear the bastard's voice.

"Listen up, Hawkins. The commander's on the line with CentCom now. I didn't tell Em this, but we've been briefed as to the conditions there. I have to be honest with you, it's not good."

No shit. "Yeah. I had kinda guessed that."

"What's your situation? Are you secure?"

"We've got nothing but two pistols among us as far as firepower. I've got five civilians holed up with me in a wood-constructed office building located in the center of the base."

Jai cleared his throat pointedly.

"One of the civilians is former military." With a glance at the photographer, Hawk amended his statement. "Another is hired muscle, so I'm pretty sure he knows his way around a gun. Two more are women and one's an Australian reporter."

"Cameraman, mate. Not a reporter, and I did some time in the Australian military myself," the Aussie corrected him.

Suddenly, it seemed everybody thought they were warriors. Hawk rolled his eyes.

He heard Dalton speaking to someone on his end of the line, then he was back. "Matt says he traced the signal from your satellite phone. He's pinpointed your precise location within the base on the GPS. Wait for us there. We're already in the air on our way to you."

So Zeta knew where they were. Great. But what the hell they thought they were going to do once they got here, Hawk couldn't even begin to guess.

"Roger that, Dalton. You got any suggestions for the meantime?"

"Just don't move from your present position until you hear from me," Dalton instructed.

Don't move? Hawk raised a brow. All of Task Force Zeta's super-secret training, all of their science-fiction-worthy state-of-the-art implants and toys, and that was the best advice Dalton could give? The same plan Hawk had already settled on before the phone call.

"Great. Thanks." Hawk shook his head and began to consider a contingency plan of his own, just in case Miller's golden boys weren't as superhuman as they thought.

"I'm sorry, Hawk. I'll get back to you. We'll have more specifics soon. Keep the phone nearby. I'll call you back."

"Copy that."

Dalton disconnected the call, leaving Hawk staring down at the black object in his hand. His fingers itched for his rifle, but instead, he was forced to depend on a damn phone and Pretty Boy Dalton and the Zetas to save him.

He was not a happy man.

"What'd they say?" The Aussie had moved to stand closer.

"To sit tight."

"I'm not too good at sitting around doing nothing, mate." Mel's proclamation sounded more like a threat.

Fists clenched, Hawk breathed in deeply through his nose, trying to control his anger. "You think I am?"

Kerri stepped between the two. She turned to Hawk and laid a hand on his forearm. "Listen, sugar. We know you're doing the best you can. If whoever was on that phone told you to sit tight, then we sit tight."

Hawk heard an irritated huff come from the corner of the office where Emily had sequestered herself since handing him the phone.

What the hell had he done to deserve this? Where the hell was his Alpha team leader? And for that matter, Wally too?

Even hung over, Wally would still be a help. Instead, Hawk was alone to deal with one inexplicably angry and obviously jealous woman, a loose-cannon cameraman and, lest he forget, a terrorist bombing and breached prison facility.

So much for his simple modeling assignment.

A camera flash brought him out of his reverie. Turning toward Rasta-photographer, Hawk frowned. "What the hell do you think you are doing?"

Camera still in hand, the man flashed brilliant, white teeth. "Recording this moment for posterity, and possibly winning me some photo awards. People love pictures of this kind of shit."

Hawk growled and was about to tell him what he thought about that when the phone rang again.

He punched the button to answer it. "Yeah."

"Hawk, it's Dalton. Listen close. We have an ETA for our arrival. This is what I need you to do. First, do not move from that building for any reason. No matter what. Do you hear me?"

"Yeah. I heard you the first time. What's the plan?"

"Can't tell you that. This isn't a secure line. You're gonna have to trust us, Hawkins."

Trust Dalton? With Emily's life and that of four other civilians currently in his care? Not a situation Hawk wanted to be in, but it looked as if he had no other choice.

"Dalton?"

"Yeah?"

"Don't screw up or I'll have to kill you."

Hawk heard his laughter through the static on the line. "Zeta doesn't screw up, Hawk. You of all people should know that."

And if Pretty Boy thought that Hawk had forgotten they were all here in Bagram and in this mess because of that stupid

183

bet made in a moment of insanity in the Alps, he was dead wrong. Hawk only hoped they all lived to regret the decision he'd made in those mountains some more tomorrow.

"Okay, Hawk, I have to go. I need you to get the civilians under as much cover as possible immediately. Stay away from the windows and doors and do not exit that building." Dalton shouted that warning again over the sound of the helo carrying Zeta to their rescue.

"Roger that."

"Tell Em she's gonna be fine. I'll be there in a few." A click and silence followed Dalton's last statement.

Phone still in his hand, Hawk glanced around the room at all of the people depending on him.

Commanding a group of soldiers was one thing. Hawk could be certain his orders would be followed. Now, he could only hope. He really hated hoping.

Pushing doubts aside, Hawk sprang into action.

"I need the men to pair off and each grab a desk. Move them to the back of the room away from the window." He grabbed the end of one desk himself as Tony quickly moved to take the other side. The two cameramen did the same with another piece of furniture.

"Everybody take cover under the desks and do not move, no matter what." He looked specifically at Emily. "Do you hear me?"

Eyes wide, she nodded and started to move just as Hawk detected the sound of Army Black Hawks in the air.

"Move it! Now. Quick."

Pinning Emily beneath the leg hole of one desk with his own body, Hawk heard the helicopters open fire as the good guys—at least he really hoped it was the good guys—blasted away, taking out the insurgents keeping them all pinned down within their own base.

No wonder Pretty Boy wanted them inside. Dalton must have located the building they were being held in and targeted any hostiles nearby. Hawk shook his head at the risky maneuver. Hitting friendlies was always a possibility in this kind of situation. Then again, Zeta had technology no normal soldier even dreamed of. Hawk and those with him were probably safer from Dalton and his guys laying down covering fire from the sky than they were from the rest of the armed personnel trying to defend the base from the bad guys already on the inside.

As Emily trembled beneath him, Hawk tucked her head beneath his chin. He mumbled against her hair, "Hell of a fucking plan, Dalton."

He hoped to God it worked.

Chapter Seventeen

The dream always hit Emily the same, never less frightening. Surreal noises came from outside the building. Even huddled beneath both the desk and Hawk's bulk, Emily was surrounded by horrible sounds the likes of which she'd only ever heard before in war movies.

Explosions, rapid gunfire, rockets whistling through the air followed by more explosions. All of that deafening, heart-stopping noise punctuated by the constant whir of helicopters above. Hawk held her tight, murmuring assurances she could barely hear over the firefight outside and her own pulse pounding.

In a cold sweat and with her heart racing, she awoke with a start. Even after all this time, months later, the recollection of those events affected her in the form of nightmares. Her memories wouldn't let her rest, day or night.

Yes, the dream always started the same. She was making her way to the USO tent to check her email just after sunrise. She caught a glimpse of Hawk, buttoning his stupid camouflage jacket while sneaking out of Kerri's tent. The realization of what must have happened between them. The feeling of nausea so strong it would have emptied her stomach if she'd taken the time to eat or drink anything that morning.

The scene usually fast-forwarded to her taking shelter beneath the desk during the melee, cradled in Hawk's arms. She hated him for what he'd done and hated herself that she couldn't bring herself to push him away. Then she'd wake up.

Maybe she needed therapy. There was no reason for her to have the nightmares. Against all odds, everyone had been rescued unharmed.

When Emily had finally heard BB's voice outside the office door, she knew everything would be all right. Two black-clad figures had broken through the flimsy wood, yelling the entire time to Hawk and Tony not to shoot, that they were the good guys.

Emily had somehow fought her way from beneath Hawk and run at BB, crashing into him hard with a hug that would have toppled a smaller man.

In the blur of shouted instructions and running that followed, before she could even begin to grasp what had happened, Emily found herself thrust into a helicopter and in the air, flying away from the battle. While the other Black Hawks above kept the men who'd attacked the base occupied, BB and his team had whisked Emily and the rest of their small group away, minus Hawk.

Hawk wasn't with them on the helicopter, nor did he arrive later while they waited in the relative safety of the airport in Kabul for word of the situation at Bagram. Unfortunately, Kerri London was there, and that was enough to remind Emily exactly why she shouldn't care if Hawk lived or died. Even more unfortunate was the fact that Emily did care what happened to Hawk. She hated that.

Glancing at her bedside clock now, she wasn't at all surprised to see it read four thirty. Why did the stupid dream always seem to come at the same time each morning? For once, she'd like to sleep at least until five thirty. Six thirty would be even better.

With a sigh, she swung her pajama-clad legs from beneath the warmth of her sheets and stumbled blindly toward the kitchen and the coffee pot. She'd learned to set up the coffee maker the night before now that the predawn awakenings had become her norm.

Yawning, Emily flipped open her laptop on the kitchen table while the steaming brew dripped slowly into the waiting carafe.

This was another habit Emily had gotten into, checking her email immediately upon waking. She did it before work each morning during the week and obsessively all day on weekends.

Worse, she'd gotten used to receiving the usual email from Hawk. She'd come to expect to find it waiting there for her. He'd emailed her nearly every day during the past months since she'd gotten home from Afghanistan. An impressive run considering she had never responded. Not even once.

How could she respond? She didn't know what to say. Her pride wouldn't allow her to admit to him that he'd torn out her heart by spending the night with Kerri. She certainly couldn't say she forgave him, because she didn't. Yet she still anticipated the correspondence daily.

He'd long since stopped begging her to tell him what had upset her that day back in Bagram—as if he didn't know. Now he simply told her about his day—the weather, funny things Wally or Pettit had said or done, apologizing profusely when a mission or an internet outage kept him from emailing her for any length of time. Each day she would read the email about twenty times and then save it in a special file to read again later.

Pitiful. That was the only word she could think of to describe this long-distance, one-sided, dead-end relationship with him. Just plain sad.

Emily rubbed her face hard with both hands, then focused her sleepy, bleary eyes on her email inbox. Frowning, she noticed that there wasn't anything new from Hawk.

Fighting the disappointment, she left the other twenty or so emails from friends, family and spammers unopened and went to the cupboard to grab a coffee mug, making excuses for the lack of word from Hawk the entire way. She'd read online yesterday that there were bad rainstorms in Afghanistan. That must be it. No internet because of the weather.

Pouring the aromatic liquid into a large ceramic cup, Emily assured herself that tomorrow, the next day at the latest, she would find an explanation and an apology from Hawk. That she'd obviously become addicted to hearing from him every day was not at all reassuring.

With a sigh, Emily carried her coffee into the bathroom. She might as well shower and get ready for the big day. Emily let out a short laugh at that thought.

It was the day of the wedding. Not her wedding, but Katie's. At least Katie and BB got to have a big day. Emily had started to doubt she ever would. Certainly not with Hawk. Most likely not at all if she didn't get over her obsession with him and move on.

She grabbed her new navy blue dress and hung it behind the bathroom door so any wrinkles would steam out while she showered.

Emily shot the offending item of clothing a dirty look as envy overwhelmed her. While she wore her stupid blue dress today, Katie would be in a long white dress.

Okay, so as pregnant as she was, Katie wouldn't be wearing a traditional white wedding dress with train and veil, but it was still a wedding dress. Katie would no doubt look beautiful in the champagne-colored, simple, chic dress. It totally suited her personality and the high empire waist accommodated her rapidly growing baby bump.

Of course Emily was happy for her friends, but she still couldn't fight the depression she felt.

Hawk was a dirty rotten bastard who had slept with another woman the same night he'd made love to her. So why couldn't Emily stop her heart from clenching each time she thought of him. If she didn't feel so miserable all the time, she'd think she was in love with him, further proof of how pitiful she was.

What had started many months ago as physical attraction and perhaps infatuation had grown into something more as she read his words in her apartment each day.

Emily shook her head. If this was love, it sucked. Perhaps she was better off without it. She was definitely better off without him. If only she could learn to actually be without him. That would never happen as long as she used his daily emails as a crutch. But the thought of never hearing from him again sent her into a heart-racing panic attack.

With her head beginning to ache from lack of sleep and too much thinking, Emily stepped beneath the stream of hot water. Hopefully it would wash away her bad mood as well as all thoughts of Hawk so she'd be able to enjoy Katie and BB's special day.

Emily needed to have her wits about her today, because after the nearly two-hour train ride to upstate New York, Emily would be serving as Katie's maid of honor. With all of BB's siblings and his team there, Emily alone would be representing Katie's side.

BB may have won the battle to have the ceremony and luncheon afterward in his hometown in New York with his massive family and his best friends from Zeta in attendance, but Katie had still managed to brutally cut down the guest list to fewer than three dozen.

Maybe from among those there, Emily would meet a nice single man who would steal her heart and make her forget all about David Hawkins.

Not likely, but she could hope.

Hawk listened, uncomfortable as his first sergeant praised his heroism before pinning the medal on his chest. A frigging medal for saving the lives of five civilians during the Bagram bombing.

The problem was, Hawk hadn't done anything. Pretty Boy Dalton and his Zeta boys had ridden in to the rescue. The most Hawk had done was relay Dalton's damn instructions from over Emily's satellite phone and then watch helplessly as they whisked Emily and the others away in the waiting helo.

Having to watch another man rescue his girl...talk about feeling impotent.

The only good thing about Zeta's dramatic rescue had been, with Emily on her way to safety, Hawk was free to run to his tent and grab his weapon. It had felt damn good to finally have the M16 in his hands and be doing something, anything, besides just sitting there. He'd found Pettit and Wally in the nearest bunker and another piece of his scrambled world settled back into place.

The Black Hawk attack had done much to rattle the insurgents within the perimeter. It hadn't taken long before they were all either captured or had fled. Hawk had helped when and where he could, always wondering about Emily's location and wellbeing until he'd finally pinned down someone affiliated with the USO who could give him confirmation she was safe.

And that was the last he'd heard about her. Not one more word in months. That was no fault of his, because he emailed her every damn day. She never once responded, but he did it anyway. Every day, he held on to some small hope that there would be a response from her. Every day, he found instead disappointment. He finally realized exactly how she had felt when he hadn't contacted her after Germany.

He'd screwed up once, but he wouldn't do it again. So he wrote every day he could. He would continue to do so until she changed her mind or he got shipped home and could see her again in person and change her mind for her.

"You don't look as happy as I thought you would, Sergeant. Something wrong?" His first sergeant draped his arm around Hawk's shoulders like they were old drinking buddies.

"This is just all a bit unexpected." Not to mention undeserved.

His commander laughed. "Most good things in life are, Sergeant."

Like meeting Emily had been.

How the hell he had managed to screw it up so badly and so suddenly, Hawk still didn't know. Being able to do nothing about it besides cool his heels for the remainder of his deployment might possibly drive him insane.

The sound of a helo in the distance captured Hawk's attention. Tensing, he frowned. It sounded like Lou's chopper, but he wasn't due in anytime soon.

He squinted at the horizon until it came into view. "Could that be mail call already? Seems like we just got it."

His first sergeant laughed. "You looking a gift horse in the mouth? Mail call and supplies can't come often enough as far as I'm concerned."

Hawk smiled. "Yeah, guess so."

Lou swooped in fast and dropped the chopper in a messy landing. He came running across the camp straight toward them.

Hawk's smile faded as instinct kicked in. "Something's wrong."

Taking off in a jog that turned into a full-out run, Hawk met the old man not far from where he'd landed.

"Lou. What's the matter?"

Wheezing with what sounded like it could be his last breath, Lou gasped. "Satellite's down. Couldn't get word to you. I came to get you." The breathless man shoved papers into Hawk's hand.

He looked down and saw the American Red Cross logo on the letterhead and his heart stopped. AmCross orders only came through when family was dying or dead and the soldier needed to get home fast. And these orders had his name on them.

Hawk was anxious to get back to the States, but not like this. He tore into the envelope and skimmed down the page. He saw his sister's name and his stomach twisted. She was the only family he had left in the world.

The first sergeant was next to him in an instant. "What's wrong?"

"My sister." Hawk looked up, still in shock. "I have to get home."

He knew that he had to move, had things to do, but he couldn't seem to function. It seemed as if his brain had stopped working.

His commander took hold of Hawk's shoulders and physically turned him back toward camp. "Go. Throw what you'll need in a duffle and get on that helo."

Chapter Eighteen

"Hey there, Emmie."

Emily glanced up from her desk as a familiar Australian voice from months past filled the room. In the doorway to her office stood the cameraman. Mel looked different, and pretty good actually, without the head-to-toe body armor and camouflage he'd worn in Bagram. He cleaned up good in boots, jeans and a white button-down shirt that set off his tanned skin.

"Mel. What are you doing here?"

"I was in New York for a job. Jai and I met nearby for a cuppa and he suggested I stop by and see you."

She was hit with a wave of nostalgia. Mel reminded her of Afghanistan and the last time she'd seen Hawk.

"So how you been, love?"

Emily shrugged. "Okay, I guess. Keeping busy."

Mel took a step closer and propped his jeans-clad butt on the edge of her desk. "Jai told me you still have dreams about the bombing."

Emily scowled. "So much for confiding in Jai."

"Don't be like that, Emmie. He and I have been through it ourselves enough to know what you're feeling. He's just concerned about you."

"I guess." She sighed.

"Well, if you need to talk, Emmie, you give me a jingle." Mel dropped a business card on her desk. "If I'm in the country, I'll come running. If not, there's always the phone or email."

She smiled. "Thanks."

"And if you wanted to give me a call to go out, I'd like that too." Mel continued, golden eyes twinkling as he smiled at her.

Emily looked up at him with surprise. "Like on a date?"

He laughed and nodded. "Unless you're still with Hawkins."

Now it was Emily's turn to laugh. "I don't know what I am."

"Well, love, I have a policy. If a woman isn't sure if she's with a man or not, that's invitation enough for me." Mel sobered and laid a hand over hers. "What's wrong, love. Someone as pretty as you shouldn't look so sad."

Mel read her too easily, and he already knew she'd slept with Hawk, so what the heck. Emily could use someone to talk to at the moment.

She let out a sigh. "The morning of the attack I saw Hawk coming out of Kerri London's tent half-dressed. Mel, he must have slept with her..." She left the rest of the horrible truth unspoken. *He slept with Kerri right after he was with me.*

Mel looked surprised. "He didn't tell you, love? Maybe not since it happened right before the bombing."

"What happened?" Emily sat up straighter in her chair.

"Pettit found Wally plonked, starkers and arse over tit with an Air Force Sheila. With Wally in the cactus, Pettit ran and got Hawk out of the shower that morning and brought him to Kerri London's tent."

Emily's heart began to pound. She didn't understand half of what he had just said, but she grasped enough to know it was important. "Mel. Please, for God's sake, could you speak English this once and tell me what happened again?"

"Sure, love." Mel grinned. "Wally was in Kerri's tent naked and drunk with the Air Force woman who was assigned as Kerri's liaison. Sex on base with a woman he outranked could get Wally in huge trouble. So Pettit ran and pulled Hawk out of the shower. That's why Hawk was coming out of Kerri's tent early in the morning half-dressed. He was trying to keep Wally from getting court marshaled."

That she understood, and it was wonderful. Wonderful and horrible at the same time. She'd ignored Hawk's emails for months because she'd made the wrong assumption. She'd tortured both him and herself rather than just ask him.

"Mel, you know all this for a fact?"

"Abso-bloody-lutely."

"I'll take that as a yes."

He nodded. "Spot on. It's a yes. Wally told me himself after I found him emptying the bourbon-soaked contents of his belly on the ground outside my tent. Pettit backed up the story. So there's no need to chuck a spaz."

"Yeah, okay." Emily couldn't interpret any more of Mel's Aussie-speak. Her mind was already on Hawk. She had to email him, but she hadn't heard from him in two weeks. What if she'd lost him? If only she could see him. If he was back in Germany maybe she could fly there, but Afghanistan...

Then another thought hit her. "Mel, I haven't gotten an email from him in two weeks. What if something happened? Can you use your connections and check?"

He frowned. "Didn't you know, love? He's here."

"What do you mean he's here? Is that some sort of slang again?" She didn't dare hope.

"No. I mean he's here in the States. Emergency leave. He told me his sister was in the hospital for emergency surgery and there were complications. He got sent home to be with her since she's his only living relative."

Emily frowned. "How do you know this?"

"He flew home through Kabul. I saw him there when he was waiting for a flight out."

A frantic feeling hit her. She had to get a message to Hawk that she was sorry before it was too late.

"I need to get on my computer. I have to look up his sister and get an address or a phone number. I have to find out where she lives. Shit, what if she's married and has a different last name? I'll never find her." Even if she wasn't married, how many Hawkins were there in the United States? Emily's head was spinning.

"Wait. I know. Katie. I'll call Katie. Maybe she can use her military connections. But she just had the baby and it's still early. I don't want to wake her up."

Mel held up a hand. "Why don't you let me see what I can do?"

Shaken and desperate, Emily nodded. She was willing to try anything.

Mel whipped out a cell phone that looked nearly as big and complicated as her laptop and punched a few buttons. He rose and walked closer to the door to speak. Curious, Emily had to fight the urge to follow him and listen in.

When a few minutes later she saw him take out a small notepad and pen, she nearly jumped from her seat.

Finally, Mel came back to her desk wearing a grin and holding a piece of paper.

"Is that—"

"His sister's address and phone number."

"How did you get it?"

"Connections, love."

Finally, Emily got up the nerve and grabbed the paper he held out for her.

"Pennsylvania?" she read.

Hawk was in Pennsylvania. So close. Only one state away. "But what if he's not still there?"

Mel shrugged. "I saw him a little less than two weeks ago. They wouldn't send him back so soon. Not counting travel time, which can take days each way, they usually give the blokes at least a solid two weeks at home for emergency leave."

Emily's hopes surged. "But wait. What if his sister died? I can't bust into her home looking for him while he's grieving. Can I? Then again, maybe he needs me now if she did—"

"Emmie, dial the bloody number or I'll do it for you."

Glancing at Mel, she predicted he would do exactly that. She took out her cell phone and dialed the number. She noticed her hands were shaking.

"Hello," a female voice answered the phone.

"Um, hi. I hate to bother you. I was actually looking for David Hawkins. I was told he might be there."

"Can I ask who's calling?"

"Um, it's Emily Price. I worked with him, not in the Army, but he did a job for my marketing company—"

"Of course, Emily. He mentioned you. I have to say, it's a pleasure to meet you, even if it is only on the phone. You're the first woman in thirty years that I've ever seen throw my brother off balance."

Emily swallowed hard. "Me? Are you sure he was talking about me?"

Hawk's sister laughed. "Yeah, pretty sure. But I'm sorry to tell you, David's gone already."

Her heart fell. "He is?"

"Yeah. He had to get back, so I've got a friend staying with me to help out until I'm totally back to one hundred percent."

"Oh. Okay. Thanks. And I hope you feel better."

"Emily, wait. He doesn't have a cell phone when he's deployed, but he checks in with me a few times a day with his calling card. Give me your number and I'll pass it along to him."

But what if he was too mad at her to call? It didn't matter. Emily had to take a shot. "Okay. Here's my work number and I'll give you my home and cell too."

Not having a cell phone never bothered Hawk while he was in Afghanistan, or even in Germany. But while in New York City trying to find Emily and having to check in with his sister often, it really sucked.

He had pretty much memorized his phone card number and was very familiar with every working pay phone in the city. And now, leaning against the tiny metal shelf, pen and scrap of paper in hand, Hawk made his third phone call in the last hour. First had been to call his captain to ask him to contact Hank Miller and get Dalton's number.

Then the call back to his captain to get the info he'd obtained from Miller. Armed with Dalton's number, he was on his hopefully final call before the only one he wanted to make— to Emily.

"I don't know about this, Hawkins. I don't feel comfortable giving Emily's information out. I mean, she never even told me you two had a history together."

After all Hawk had gone through, Pretty Boy had the nerve to question his intentions toward Emily like he was her damn father. "Well, we do."

"Maybe as far as you're concerned. But Emily—"

Hawk took a deep breath to steady his temper. "Look, Dalton. I've still got more than half of my time left to serve in Afghanistan. I'm here in the States for another two days and then I'm gone again. But I'll be back here as soon as Uncle Sam lets me. I'm not looking for a one-night stand."

If Emily still wanted him, that is. Actually, fuck that. Even if she didn't, he wouldn't leave her alone until he changed her mind.

Dalton remained silent. Hawk was about to give up on this call. He could try to find a computer to email her. He decided to give it one more try.

"I want to build a future with her, but first I need to know where to find her."

"All right. Got a pen?"

Thank God, he'd finally given in. Hawk scribbled the info Dalton relayed. "Um, I wouldn't mind knowing how big a battle this is going to be either. I mean, if she's seeing someone else."

Shit, that could be why she hadn't responded to any of his emails.

Dalton laughed. "You're really pushing it, Hawk. Fine, I don't think I am spilling any secrets if I tell you she attended my wedding alone. She was invited with a date but she chose not to bring one."

Hawk would take anything he could get. His hope renewed, he was totally sincere when he said, "Thanks, Dalton."

"You're welcome. But I have to tell you one thing."

"What's that?"

"Emily is like my sister. You hurt her and I'm going to have to do something about it."

Hawk laughed, figuring that if they really wanted to, Pretty Boy and the Zetas could probably do all sorts of things to him and get away with it. Luckily, they seemed like a peaceable group, when not dealing with insurgents, that was.

"I hear you, Dalton. I'd never willingly hurt her." Although, somehow, someway, he'd managed to do something that had upset her enough she'd frozen him out of her life. Now that he was here, he fully intended to find out what and fix it.

Hawk wasn't all that familiar with Manhattan, but if he could find his way through the mountain paths of Afghanistan while being shot at, he figured he could navigate New York City. The streets were numbered after all.

One quick question to a passing man in a suit and Hawk knew which direction Madison Avenue was. He had no problem finding the address Dalton had given him for Emily's office building. Soon he stood in front of it, his heart pounding at the thought of seeing Emily again.

This whole trip could be a waste of time. Then again, it might not be. Determined, he pushed through the glass doors and into the lobby.

A quick elevator trip upstairs and he was walking through the office door, shaking but determined. Then there stood Emily, right in front of him and holding an obviously newborn baby.

Holy shit.

The first thought that assaulted Hawk, that nearly took him down to his knees, was that he'd gotten Emily pregnant that first time they'd had sex in Germany. But wait. That wasn't nine months ago and they'd used protection.

The second thought was that Emily having a baby was one piece of information Dalton could have let him know about during that phone call.

Had she been pregnant with another man's child both times they'd been together? She hadn't looked it in Afghanistan, but it would explain why she wouldn't email him back.

It must have been obvious to Emily by his expression that he was counting backward and trying to reason this out. Once the look of shock that had appeared when she saw him standing in the doorway finally left Emily's face, she shook her head.

"Don't worry. This is Katie and BB's baby. Not mine. Or yours."

He itched to tell her when he thought about having kids the only woman he could picture having them with was her. Instead, he took a step forward and peeked at the infant's face. "Pretty little thing. She looks like her father."

"He looks like his father. It's a boy."

Hawk raised one eyebrow. "That figures." Even Dalton's son was pretty.

Emily walked to some sort of stroller thing, gently laid the baby down, covered him with a pale blue blanket and jingled some plastic colored toys that hung in front of his face. When she returned to Hawk, she looked uncomfortable.

"So I guess your sister told you I called."

"My sister?" He shook his head. "I haven't spoken to my sister yet today."

"Then how did you know where I work?"

"I tracked down Dalton and asked where to find you. I figured he owed me one."

Before she could respond to that, two men and a redheaded female came out of a back room.

The woman arched one eyebrow in surprise when she saw him. "Sergeant Hawkins. A pleasure to finally meet you." She stepped forward and extended her hand. "Katie Dalton."

"My boss," Emily added.

And Dalton's wife. Well, hell. Hawk didn't realize Pretty Boy had it in him to choose a mature, sexy businesswoman for a wife. He'd pictured him more with some model-type bimbo.

"Hawk. Our Army man. Of course, I didn't recognize you in civilian clothing." The older of the two men moved forward, one beefy arm extended.

"These are the owners of the agency. That's James Howard and his partner, Morris Dean." Emily made the introductions.

Hawk shook hands with both men as the thinner of the two, Morris Dean, asked, "What brings you to our neck of the woods? Or more accurately, the concrete jungle of New York?"

No use lying about it. "I came to see Emily."

Dalton's wife looked very interested as she glanced from Hawk to Emily and back. "Well, it's good to meet you. Em, why don't you take the rest of the day to show our new star around the city."

"Good idea. In fact, take him down to Times Square and stand him in front of that billboard with his ad on it. That should raise some public interest, don't you think?" James Howard asked his partner.

The other man bobbed his head in agreement. "Definitely. Great idea, Jim. A shame he's not in uniform, but the tourists might still recognize him. Do you need the company limo, Emily?"

Emily looked shocked by the offer. "Um. No, thanks, I think we'll be fine walking. It's a nice day. I'll just grab my jacket."

Just outside the office door, as they waited in awkward silence for the elevator to arrive, Hawk turned to Emily. "I might have enjoyed the limo."

Looking miserable, she ignored his joke. "Hawk, we need to talk. There's something I need to say."

He wasn't sure if that was good news or bad news. Talking was better than not, he supposed, unless of course what she had to say was leave her alone or she'd get a restraining order. "Okay. Is there someplace we can go for some privacy?"

Times Square in front of his billboard wasn't where he wanted to be for this ominous conversation—and no one had told him he'd be on a frigging billboard anyway.

"Privacy is pretty hard to find here in Manhattan." Her throat worked as she swallowed and glanced up at him. "But my apartment isn't too far."

Her apartment. Damn, he wanted her so badly he could barely stand it. "Okay. Let's go to your place then...if you don't mind."

Hawk held his breath and waited.

"No. It's fine. It's even clean. I've, uh, been waking up early so I clean before work."

They both remained mostly silent during the cab ride to her apartment, making the trip seem eternally long. When they finally arrived, she fumbled with her key in the door.

She walked through the door, turned to him and began speaking at the same moment he did.

"Hawk. I'm so sorry—"

"Emily, I don't know what I did, but—" Hawk stopped his apology when he realized she was apologizing to him. "Wait. What are you sorry about?"

She took a deep breath and glanced into the tiny living room. "Can we sit?"

They could stand on their heads for all he cared, as long as she was finally ready to discuss the two of them.

Hawk wanted to clear the air, the sooner the better. He'd been through too many days and nights of agony already. "Okay. Let's sit."

They moved farther into the room and he dropped his duffle to the floor. It was strange getting a glimpse into her world. Until now, she'd been on his turf. Her laughably tiny city apartment felt as foreign to him as Afghanistan probably had to her.

Seated on the couch that barely fit the two of them, Emily angled her body toward his. "I made an assumption, an incorrect assumption it turns out. I should have confronted you about it right away. Instead, I acted like a child not emailing you back."

"I don't understand. What assumption?"

"I saw you coming out of Kerri London's tent the morning of the bombing at Bagram. I assumed you'd—"

"Had sex with her? Right after I'd been with you?" Hawk sat in shock. "Emily. What the hell kind of man do you think I am?"

"It was barely dawn. You were half dressed. I—" Her eyes filled with tears. "I know. I'm so sorry. It's just, I was so hurt."

Hawk let out a frustrated breath as he gathered her against him. She came willingly into his arms. "You were hurting over nothing. I can't believe you spent all this time thinking I would do that to you when all you had to do was ask me."

"I would have said something that morning, but then there was the explosion."

He remembered. She had started to say something and then all hell had broken loose. Shaking his head, he squeezed her closer. All those months of agony on both their parts.

"I was getting one of my men out of Kerri's tent. That's all."

"I know. Mel told me when I saw him."

"Mel?" That name rang a bell. Hawk froze as he put the name with the man. "Crocodile Cameraman?"

Emily nodded, laughing tearfully at the nickname. "Yeah."

How the fuck could he be here in New York? Hawk had just seen him when he flew out of Kabul to get home to his sister.

"So you saw Mel?" The ugly green monster inside Hawk reared its ugly head.

"This morning. He was meeting Jai and stopped by to say hello."

Who the fuck was Jai? Then Hawk remembered Rasta-photographer.

"He told me he'd seen you, then he told me about you having to get Wally out of Kerri's tent."

Hawk frowned. "So do you see this Mel often?"

Emily pulled back and looked at him. "You're jealous."

"No." Hawk sighed then opted for the truth. He'd do anything, even admit this, if it would keep Emily in his life. "Yes. I've never been so jealous of any man in my entire life."

Of course, he'd probably never felt as much for any woman as the way he did about Emily. "He was all over you in Bagram, Emily."

Emily smiled. "It was an act to make you jealous."

"You were doing it on purpose?"

"Not really." She shrugged. "It was all Mel's doing, but I kind of went along with it."

Relief overwhelmed him, along with curiosity. Although he suspected he knew the answer to his next question. "Why?"

"Because I was jealous of you being with that flirty Kerri London every second of the day."

That was what he had hoped. Hawk laughed and pulled her closer again. "We make a hell of a pair."

They could maybe even be happy if they both stopped getting in their own way.

Emily looked up at him with baby blues that could melt a man. She leaned in. "Kiss me?"

With a groan, he tangled his hand in her hair. "You don't have to ask me twice."

Hawk crashed his mouth into hers. He'd intended to be gentle, but the pent-up passion of the past months without her rose to the surface. It poured into his kiss as he angled his head and thrust his tongue against hers. He'd needed her so badly and for so long.

They had to make enough memories to hold him for the rest of his deployment.

Wanting nothing between them, Hawk tugged at Emily's clothes. She had far too much on. He peeled off layer after layer. Suit jacket, shoes, pants and blouse. He revealed her inch-by-inch until she was in nothing but bits of lace covering the key areas he was anxious to get to.

He needed her more with each new exposed portion of her creamy skin. Hawk slid his hands over her body, her curves both familiar and new to him at the same time. They'd only been together twice, once for the night, and once for just a few stolen moments, but he'd remember both times forever.

And now she was here and it was time to create new memories.

Tasting her, caressing her, kissing the warm soft flesh was better than any of his dreams. Her lips had never tasted sweeter, her body had never felt more responsive than at this moment.

This time seemed to be so much more than the other times they'd been together. Perhaps because he felt so much more for her now. He'd almost lost her because he hadn't let her know just how he felt. How deep his feelings for her ran.

He'd never make that mistake again. This time he'd leave her with no doubt of how much she meant to him, how much he needed her.

But now wasn't the time to talk. Not when his mouth had so many better things to do.

After a struggle to get out of his jeans and button-down shirt, Hawk finally freed himself. He pulled a nearly naked Emily onto his lap. She straddled him, facing him so he had access to everything he craved. He pushed aside the white lace of her bra and drew one taut, pink nipple into his mouth. She trembled above him.

Slipping his hand into her panties, he found her wet from wanting him. That knowledge drew a groan from deep inside him.

Burying his face against her as he took in her warm scent, Hawk pushed aside her panties and slid his fingers inside her. The feeling of her heat almost mind-blowing, he plunged into her again and again.

She rocked against his hand as he worked her clit, shaking, gasping, making those tiny noises that drove him insane as she came closer to release.

Thank God, he'd been bold enough to bring a condom, just in case. Stretching until he nearly fell off the couch with her in his lap, he reached his pants and the foil packet in the pocket. He covered himself and then guided Emily over him.

He slid in easily. They were both more than ready for this. She rode him until he felt the muscles inside her gripping him so tightly he thought he'd lose his mind.

As he felt her orgasm breaking, he thrust her down onto his cock one last time as he exploded inside her.

Still breathless, he shook his head. "I'll last longer next time. I swear. It's just...it's been a while."

"I'm glad to hear that."

"Which part?"

"Both." She smiled. Then the smile faded. "When do you have to leave?"

"Two days." Too soon.

"Are you going back to your sister's tonight?"

"Nope. But I'll have to find someplace to stay. Maybe a hotel or something." He grinned, knowing what she'd say.

Her eyes opened wide. "You will not. You're staying here."

"I was hoping you'd say that." He leaned in for another taste of her mouth, then a thought hit him. "Wait. You said you called my sister? How? She still goes by her ex-husband's last name."

She smiled. "Mel. He got her number somehow."

Hawk cocked a brow. "Oh really."

Mel's involvement in their reconciliation didn't make him happy, but that Emily had been trying to reach him sure did. All at the same time that he was trying to get to her through Dalton.

He kissed Emily, claiming her mouth with enough force she'd forget all about Mel and everything else. When he finally pulled back, he had only one question. "So when I get back to the FOB and I email you, you going to email back?"

She grabbed his face in her hands. "So often you're going to get sick of me."

"Not gonna happen." Hawk shook his head. "I'll never get sick of you."

Teary-eyed, Emily smiled. "Good."

So many twists of fate had brought them together, all the way back to that first day on the mountain in the Alps. It was like the universe was telling them, over and over again, they were meant to be together. For once, Hawk was going to listen.

About the Author

As an award-winning author of contemporary erotic romance in genres including military, cowboy, and menage, Cat Johnson uses her computer so much she wore the letters off the keyboard within a year. She is known for her creative marketing and research practices. Consequently, Cat owns an entire collection of camouflage and western attire for book signings and a fair number of her consultants wear combat or cowboy boots for a living. In her real life, she's been a marketing manager, professional harpist, bartender, tour guide, radio show host, Junior League president, sponsor of a bull-riding rodeo cowboy, wife and avid animal lover.

To learn more about Cat, please visit www.catjohnson.net. Send an email to Cat at cat@catjohnson.net, like her Facebook page at www.facebook.com/CatJohnsonAuthor or follow her on Twitter at @cat_johnson.

He has met the enemy...but he's never fought desire like this.

A Few Good Men
© *2012 Cat Johnson*
Red, Hot, & Blue, Book 7

Deployed in the deadliest place on earth, Army Staff Sergeant John Blake relies on caffeine, adrenaline, years of training and sheer force of will to get through his days. He has no problem with his tank crew passing around a sexy romance novel, but John's a fighter, not a lover. He'll pass.

Winding up as the author's accidental pen pal wasn't in his plan, but there's something about her sweet, caring emails that have him looking forward to checking his inbox.

Week after week, Maureen Mullen, aka erotic romance writer Summer Winters, has dated one loser after another in a quest to find the last decent man on earth. Now it seems she's found him—halfway around the world. When it comes to falling for unavailable men, she's batting a thousand.

Gradually, the emails between the war-hardened warrior and the writer of passionate prose heat up to the point of keeping them up warm and wanting at night. Soon they're wondering if it's possible to build something solid out of cyberspace, or if it's just an emotional mirage that will dissolve in the heat of reality.

Warning: Contains some steamy phone calls from the war zone and one hell of a sexy first meeting between two strangers who are already in love.

Available now in ebook and print from Samhain Publishing.

*When it comes to love, sometimes
a girl has to go above and beyond.*

In the Line of Duty
© *2012 Donna Alward*
First Responders, Book 2

Jake Symonds has been a thorn in Constable Kendra Givens's side since the night they first met, when she'd had to arrest him. In his boxer shorts. The drunken comments he made that night are worsened by the truth she'll never admit. For a fleeting moment, they'd connected.

Two years later, when she's called to investigate a break-and-enter at his pub, the last thing she expects is for the now-competent businessman to cook her breakfast. But she's no fool. The former bad boy still lurks beneath the charm. And his business involves the one thing that she's hated since it ruined her childhood. Alcohol.

As far as he's concerned, Jake has changed, but Kendra still has a stick up her butt. Yet he can't help but like her sass and quick wit. One well-aimed baseball at the carnival dunk tank later and he's got a date.

Their spark of attraction quickly flares out of control, but their emotional baggage is stacked too high to risk anything deeper—until one tragic night strips the barriers from their deepest fears. And Kendra realizes the greatest danger Jake presents is to her heart.

Warnings: Readers should be aware that any sexy comments made to police officers will be used against them in the hottest way possible.

Available now in ebook from Samhain Publishing.

11/17 (6) 5/16

CPSIA information can be obtained at www.ICGtesting.com
Printed in the USA
LVOW07s2203301213

367533LV00004B/294/P

9 781619 215153